MIDNIGHT STRIKES

TOM REYNOLDS

ONE

It was just before dawn and Midnight was as ready as he'd ever be. He'd been lying in wait, literally, for an hour now. The concrete beneath him could have been a pillow and it would have felt the same through his tactical armor, but his elbows were stiff from holding the binoculars to his face for so long. He had considered not wearing the armor tonight. If he was wrong, it would do little to stop him from getting killed. Without it, the increase in mobility might give him a fighting chance. Ultimately, he'd decided that if the armor stopped even one blow from Jones, it would be worth the added bulk.

If Midnight was right, Jones had been holed up in a penthouse apartment high above Empire City for months. He still didn't know for certain despite a never-ending series of stakeouts, but his gut told him this was the place. The penthouse belonged to a foreign oligarch who had bought it to launder international black market income. Despite its price tag and the outstanding view of the city skyline, its owner hadn't visited in nearly five years. Not that this was so unusual. Empire City had suffered more than most cities from the emergence of metahumans.

Midnight moved silently into position. The first rays of daylight would soon creep over the horizon, robbing Midnight of the advantage darkness always gave. He doubted Jones had any security that would warn him of Midnight's position, but that didn't mean there weren't cameras and motion sensors leftover from the penthouse's previous tenant.

In all the time Jones had spent terrorizing cities around the world, he had never spoken a word. Many took that, coupled with his appetite for destruction, as a sign of his lack of intelligence. Midnight knew not to underestimate the quiet ones.

To Midnight's right was a hardened aluminum case. He threw it open without taking his eyes off the penthouse. Inside the case was what looked like a rifle capable of taking down an elephant, except the muzzle looked like it had more in common with a piece of lab equipment than a weapon of war. The opposite end consisted of metal coils and a thick glass tube. Midnight flipped several mechanical switches along the barrel of the device, checking a series of LED numerical readouts against a list attached to the gauntlet on his left forearm.

Satisfied, he hoisted the device out of its case, rested it against his shoulder, and flipped a switch next to the sight of the weapon. He placed his right eye over the sight and saw the world through a multicolored heat reading. The weapon's scope didn't have the same advanced capabilities as his dedicated binoculars, but it picked up the vague outline of a person registering at around ninety-eight degrees Fahrenheit in the apartment across the street.

The device had been Midnight's obsession since

metahumans first appeared. He'd needed a way to stop the metahumans who became a threat to others and themselves. Rigging the weapon on his shoulder had taken longer than he'd imagined, and he intended to use the weapon to even the odds once and for all.

While Midnight was certain the device worked, he wasn't so confident about its harmful side effects. He also wasn't sure how permanent its effects would be. He was reasonably sure the weapon wouldn't disable Jones's meta-bands for good, but he hadn't tested this hypothesis on another metahuman first. He had hoped to find a metahuman with relatively benign powers to act as a willing guinea pig, perhaps in exchange for a new set of metabands procured on the black market, but Midnight had run out of time.

If the numbers he had run were correct and Jones's powers were indeed tied to the rest time between use, then the entire city was in grave danger. The weapon's first test would have to be a field one. If it didn't work, there could be trouble, but if he continued to sit back and let Jones's power grow, the entire world, and not just Empire City, would be in danger.

Midnight looked down the scope at the warm blob of pixels inside the apartment and considered taking his shot, when his communicator chirped in his ear.

"Incoming transmission fro—" the computerized female artificial intelligence voice began before being cut off. An urgent voice, no less familiar to Midnight, replaced the AI's soft, pleasant-sounding one.

"What the hell are you doing?" The Governor yelled through Midnight's earpiece.

Midnight had granted the metahuman access to his comms for emergencies. Midnight regretted not pushing harder for permission to track The Governor through the earpiece. He had no idea whether The Governor was on the other side of the globe or standing right behind him. Given more time, he could override a few settings to get a general idea of where The Governor was calling from, but Midnight didn't have any extra time lying around.

He considered ignoring the call and the question, but The Governor already knew Midnight had received the transmission. If the transmission had failed, The Governor would have received a warning letting him know the earpiece had been knocked loose and Midnight was potentially in trouble.

Against his better judgment, Midnight responded.

"There's no time to wait. I've found Jones and the weapon works. I'm won't pass up this chance just to have him go on another killing spree before we get another shot. I'm taking him down once and for all," Midnight told The Governor, his focus on the building never shifting.

"You have no idea if your weapon works," The Governor responded. "This is reckless and you know it. If you're wrong..."

"I'm not."

"Then wait for me. We'll take him down together, like we should have a long time ago."

Midnight showed no outward signs of considering The Governor's proposition, but internally, he was torn. The Governor was right—there were no guarantees—but after months of searching for Jones, he had invested too much time and effort to risk having him slip away again.

"Please, just wai—"

Midnight turned off his comm. It pained him to do it. The Governor was an ally. More than an ally. He was a friend. He cared about Midnight, which made it so much harder to ignore his plea. He was trying to protect Midnight from himself, and not for the first time.

The Governor was no doubt on his way to Midnight's location, having ascertained it through other means since he already knew Midnight's plan. The fact The Governor had pleaded with Midnight to wait meant he wasn't close and Midnight could complete his mission and incapacitate Jones before The Governor arrived. But there were few places on earth that The Governor couldn't reach within minutes. If Midnight was going to go after Jones, now was the time.

He took a deep breath, steadied his hand, and pulled the trigger.

The device discharged soundlessly. The only indication that anything had happened was a small light on the device's side that changed from green to red. The heat signature of the person inside also changed. Its temperature reading slowly fell, and for the first time since Midnight began observing it, the figure moved. It stood and walked across the room.

Now was Midnight's chance.

He quickly lowered the device from his shoulder and began detaching wires and unlatching components. He silently cursed himself for not designing a more modular device, but as with everything else about this mission, he'd had too little time.

After a few frustrating seconds, Midnight freed the piece he needed from the tangled mess of wires and circuitry. He wrapped one hand around the mechanical piece and unclipped the grappling gun from his belt with the other. In one fluid movement, he took aim and fired a line across the street. The grapple's anchor sailed through the early morning darkness in silence until it reached the floor-to-ceiling window of the penthouse. Then shards of broken glass tumbled down onto the empty streets below in a tremendous crash.

Midnight flipped a switch on the grappling gun with his thumb. The butt of the gun released a small explosion that drove a metal anchor deep into the edge of the rooftop he stood on. A small motor pulled the wire taut between the two buildings, and Midnight was off, sliding down the wire toward the penthouse, the device tucked under his arm like a football.

With the window already gone, Midnight gracefully tumbled into the living room of the penthouse. Upon landing, he quickly planted the device into the floor. A system designed around the same principle as his grappling gun went to work. A series of four metal arms drove anchors into the floor, shattering the tile beneath.

The device now secure, Midnight slammed his hand down on the flashing green button on top of the device, indicating it was once again ready to discharge. This time, there was a more noticeable effect, and the lights inside the penthouse dimmed as the energy released. The ambient hum of the apartment's electrical system went quiet, and Midnight stood in the seemingly deserted penthouse. The only noise was the wind blowing through the missing window pane and the distant sound of the remaining glass shards hitting the street below.

"Jones!" Midnight shouted down the hallway toward the center of the apartment.

Silence.

Midnight stepped over the device and headed down the hall. He flipped his cowl's visor back to thermal imaging and saw a figure standing in the middle of a room at the end of the hallway.

"It's all over, Jones. That sound you heard was a

temporal pulse. Your abilities won't work. Step out and make this easy on both of us."

There was no response, not that Midnight was expecting one. If he'd thought any of this would go down easy, he wouldn't have waited so long.

The door leading to the room with the thermal silhouette was ajar, which worried Midnight more than if it'd been made of reinforced steel and sealed shut. He inched closer until it was within reach, then he leaned in and gently pushed the door open.

Inside, the room was empty except for a man in an all-white suit with his back to Midnight.

"Turn around, Jones," Midnight shouted.

The man began to turn.

"Slowly," Midnight clarified.

This was it. After all this time, after so many needless deaths and so much destruction, Jones was in front of Midnight. He had him.

Jones faced Midnight, his expression eerily blank as always. His eyes were focused on a random spot in the middle of the room. He barely even registered that Midnight was in the room with him.

"Show me your hands," Midnight ordered, keeping his hands up in front of him, ready for a fight.

Jones raised his hands.

The order to show his hands had nothing to do with a fear that Jones may be concealing a weapon. Jones was the weapon. Midnight's demand was solely about the metabands.

"Put your arms out," Midnight ordered.

Jones complied. As he raised his arms from his sides, the sleeves of his suit receded, and Midnight finally got a good look at his metabands.

The bands were glowing, pulsating even. But it wasn't light that surrounded them; it was darkness—the darkest shade of black Midnight had ever seen. It didn't even register as a color. Instead, it was like staring into a black hole. Midnight seldom felt fear, he'd long ago trained himself to put the emotion aside, but he felt it now.

"Power those down," Midnight ordered.

Jones brought his hands up to his chest and gently clicked the metabands together, but the metabands did not change in appearance. They were neither powered on nor turned off.

In a moment of panic caused by his general uncertainty of everything he was witnessing, Midnight reached out to grab the metabands around Jones's wrists, hoping they had powered off when Jones had brought them together like every other pair of metabands in existence did. Before Midnight could wrap his gloved fingers around the metabands, Jones moved.

The movement was swift. His eyes suddenly focused on Midnight as he brought his right foot up to Midnight's chest.

The blow caught Midnight off guard. The second blow came a fraction of a second later and threw Midnight across the room. His back hit the wall. It had all happened so quickly. He was disorientated, the air firmly knocked out of his lungs.

He struggled to get his feet back under him, his back pressed against the wall for support. His eyes never left Jones, but Jones remained motionless, his gaze again unfocused.

Either Midnight's device had worked, or Jones was toying with him. Midnight wouldn't have survived a direct hit like that from a fully powered-up Jones. At full power,

Jones would have been pulling his foot out of a hole in Midnight's chest.

Midnight shook the cobwebs from his head and moved his hand to a pouch on the side of his belt. He removed a small metal rod and brought it up to his face, fumbling slightly to engage the hidden mechanism. Once engaged, the rod telescoped out to roughly two feet long. At either end were heavy-duty versions of the type of zip ties used in riot arrests.

Midnight often used the device to apprehend metahumans who refused to forfeit their powered-down bands. It prevented a person from reactivating their metabands while in custody, before they could be coerced into removing them. If they refused, a more permanent lock could be applied at a detention facility.

"It's over, Jones," Midnight said, now back on his feet. "Your metabands aren't going to work anymore. There's no way out. If you don't let me take you in, I can't guarantee what someone else might do to you once they find you. Other metahumans are likely already on their way here to put you down for good. This is your only chance."

Without a word, Jones raised his arms again. Midnight didn't hesitate this time and moved swiftly to place the restraints around his wrists before Jones could surprise him again.

"Good. Very good," Midnight said, relieved that the restraints were now in place, but he was still cautious.

He took his eyes off Jones for an instant to look down at the touch panel embedded into the forearm of his suit, intending to call in a metahuman response team to take Jones into custody.

But that instant was all Jones needed. He took a single step and swung his weight forward. His forehead smashed into the bridge of Midnight's nose. Even with carbon fiber reinforcement in his mask, his nose broke instantly. He hurried to put distance between himself and Jones the best way he knew how: with a fist.

Midnight's punch landed hard. Jones tumbled across the room and landed in a heap. Midnight wiped at his eyes, clearing the tears caused by the broken nose.

"Is that what you want? You want to make this difficult? You do not want to fight me one on one. You will lose, Jones, and I won't hold back from killing you if I have to."

Jones rose to his feet. He struggled to bring his shackled hands up to his face and wipe a sleeve across his mouth. The pristine white sleeve came back streaked with red. Jones's eyes widened at the sight. It had been a long time since he had seen his own blood. And for the first time Midnight saw a flash of emotion on his face. Rage.

Jones coiled like a mountain lion and launched himself at Midnight, eyes wild with fury. Midnight rolled to the side, avoiding the attack. Jones landed where Midnight had stood an instant before and slid across the hardwood floor. He recovered quicker than Midnight and leaped onto his back. In the blink of an eye, he had his right arm around Midnight's neck. He leveraged it against his other arm and applied pressure. Midnight could feel the flow of blood being cut off from his brain and needed to move fast before he blacked out.

He used Jones's own body weight as a counter and threw the maniac over his shoulder. This did nothing to loosen Jones's grip, and Midnight tumbled clumsily on top of Jones, his back to Jones's front. Midnight squirmed as Jones struggled to tighten his grip on his throat. As Jones readjusted his grip, Midnight lifted his head and brought it back down as hard as he could with the limited space. The blow loosened Jones's grip, and he didn't hesitate to get back on his feet, panting as his face returned to a more natural shade of color.

Jones struggled back onto his feet too, his back to Midnight. When he turned to face him, his mouth and chin were covered in blood. He wiped his sleeve across his face and again observed the red streak it came away with. He looked confused. The corner of his mouth turned up as he tried to comprehend what he was seeing, revealing a mouth full of broken teeth.

"Your powers aren't working," Midnight said between breaths. "Stop. We don't have to do this. You don't have to lose your life, and I do not want to take it. Please, just stand down. Let's finally end this."

Jones glared at Midnight. He looked around the empty room, considering his options. For a moment, Midnight thought he might have him, that he might actually surrender. Nothing would have made him happier, but Jones wasn't going to let that happen today.

Jones turned and ran. It seemed foolish, the idea of outrunning Midnight without his powers and with no place to go, and for this reason, Midnight hesitated. He thought there was no place to run, but he'd forgotten about the window his grappling line had smashed. The window that offered a ten-foot-tall opening to the rest of the world, eighty-nine stories below.

Realizing this was where Jones was headed, Midnight gave chase. He slammed into the wall of the hallway as he took the turn, but he recovered and kept running. He retrieved his grappling gun from his belt, reloaded it, took aim, and fired. The grapple exploded from the gun, followed by a line of carbon fiber paracord strong enough to haul a small car.

But Jones didn't hesitate when he reached the abyss, and the grapple arrived too late to catch him. The shot sailed out into the early morning sky before succumbing to gravity and falling.

Midnight cursed and broke into a sprint, heading for the nonexistent window. At the edge, he didn't hesitate either.

The fall was long but would be over, one way or another, in a matter of seconds. Midnight pulled his arms in, making his body into an aerodynamic projectile, though catching up with Jones would be difficult.

Jones's powers would only be disrupted temporarily. He had hit him with a concentrated pulse and set up a dome of interference inside the apartment, using the highest wattage power supply he could get his hands on, but the effects wouldn't extend far beyond the apartment's perimeter.

Somehow, Jones understood this. Midnight wasn't sure how much of a real human being was left rattling around in Jones's head. Maybe he was acting on instinct, but whatever it was, Jones felt the need to get as far away from Midnight's device as possible. Midnight had seconds, if that, to get Jones back inside the perimeter before his powers returned.

The grappling gun was still in Midnight's hand as he fell. He grabbed another cartridge containing a small hook and line from his belt and inserted it into the gun. With no time to spare, this was the only shot he'd get. He quickly aimed and pulled the trigger. This time, his targetting was perfect. The hook found its target and wrapped around Jones's body several times, pinning his arms to his sides. There was no chance he would wiggle free while powerless.

Midnight adjusted a dial on his grappling gun as he turned over in midair, hoping the flat surface of his back would offer enough wind resistance to give him an extra half a second before he was turned into street pizza. He wouldn't have time to load another cartridge, not that he had a cartridge left anyway.

But it was okay. If Midnight was going to die today, at least he'd have died while bringing down Jones. The other end of the line would anchor at the edge of the apartment's window before recoiling at high speed, bringing the entwined Jones back inside the device's range and stalling the return of his powers. He would be helpless, tied up and stranded against the building. By now, someone would have called 911. In minutes, a response team would arrive on the scene and take in the powerless Jones. He would never hurt another person again. *My life is a small price to pay*, he thought to himself as he fell.

Just as Midnight was about to squeeze the trigger, there was a bright flash, followed by a sudden change in momentum that put several G's worth of strain on his body. Then it was over, and Midnight was standing on solid ground.

He didn't recognize his surroundings right away, but they were familiar. Warehouses, factories, a small patch of grass on a field of dirt. And he wasn't alone.

"I'm sorry, Midnight," Silk said.

"What have you done?" Midnight asked her, spinning in place to get a read on exactly where he was and how far away she had flown him.

"The Governor sent me. He's on his way, but he told me to get you out of there before Jones ripped your head off your shoulders," she said.

A red blur streaked over their heads toward the city's skyline, followed by a sonic boom. It was The Governor.

"Take me back there now!" Midnight barked at Silk.

"I can't do that, Midnight. I can't bring you back there just to get yourself killed," she replied.

"You need to bring me back now. There's no time!"

And in a flash, she was gone.

Midnight turned back toward the Empire City skyline in the distance, just in time to see the eighty-nine-story apartment building fall over sideways and tumble to the ground.

TWO

ONE YEAR LATER

It was nighttime outside of one of the most rundown, grungy pawnshops in the city, and that was saying something in a city full of rundown, grungy pawnshops. It had been on Simon's radar for some time, even before The Battle of Empire City a year prior. The place had dealt in metahuman-related goods back when it was still mostly legal and, more importantly, back when metahumans still existed.

Those who desperately wished to become metahumans, or those who wanted to keep metahumans away, were drawn in by ridiculous promises about the junk sold there. Crystals, amulets, serums—it was all useless crap designed to trick the desperate.

But since it had a reputation for dealing in these types of goods, it was possible they might stumble onto legitimate relics. If you had a piece of debris from The Battle or a found pair of nonfunctional metabands, this was the place you would try to sell them to avoid getting arrested.

A year had passed since Simon had worn Midnight's cowl. There wasn't much of a reason to anymore. His primary concern was retrieving what he'd lost during The Battle, although he knew he would never find much of it again. The device that had temporarily rendered Jones powerless was still out there somewhere, though.

In a world without metahumans, the device was all but worthless. Nevertheless, it belonged to Simon, and he wanted it back. Although he doubted a person buying it secondhand from a thrift store could decipher any of the technology inside, he would feel better having it back in his hands.

Simon walked up to the pawnshop. Steel bars covered its front door to keep people from breaking in while the store was closed. The owner kept a shotgun under the counter to make sure no one caused trouble while it was open.

Before, he'd dress head to toe in black to hide in the shadows. Now, he had to hide in plain sight. He kept his blond hair short and wore nondescript clothing: a pair of jeans, no-name boots, a button-down work shirt, a black jacket, and gloves. He purposefully bought unflattering, ill-fitting clothing that didn't accentuate his physique. He did not want to stand out in any way.

This wasn't only to stay in the shadows, but also out of necessity. Federal and local governments wanted to question Midnight about what had happened before and during The Battle, which had leveled much of the city. He wanted to cooperate and help, but anything he told them would only confuse them further. They couldn't change the outcome, so as far as Simon was concerned, information about the events that had led to The Battle was useless to the authorities.

Simon pushed through the store's front door and entered the dingy, overly crowded shop. Every corner was packed to the brim with junk, none of which seemed to be organized in any perceivable way.

"Can I help you?" the man behind the counter asked.

His name was Grady Mitchell. Simon had already done his research. His long gray hair was pulled into a tight pony-tail. He wore olive green army fatigues that were frayed around the edges.

"Just browsing," Simon replied, picking up a used toaster from the nearest shelf and pretending to give it a once-over.

Intel on the interior of the shop had been scarce, leaving Simon with no choice but to visit the store. He avoided this type of investigation whenever possible. It made it much harder to fly under the radar. People always left a trail when they visited a place.

Simon didn't expect to find what he was looking for on any of the shelves, but this kind of place would have it. On the other side of the store, a customer riffled through a stack of old stereo equipment.

"Are you sure you don't have any other amplifiers?" the man asked the shop owner.

"Positive. Everything we have is on the floor."

The customer looked disappointed. He gave the few audio items stacked on the floor one last glance and left.

The store was empty now, meaning Simon had to act before some random passerby strolled in to look at the wares.

He approached the back counter and said, "I'm looking for something a little unusual."

"Like I told the last guy, anything we have for sale is already on the floor. If it ain't out there, I ain't got it," the shop owner replied.

"What I'm looking for isn't the kind of stuff you'd keep

out on the shelves."

Simon floated it out there like a test balloon to see how the man would react.

As he'd expected, the man neither signaled that he knew what Simon was talking about nor proclaimed his ignorance. He simply stared, leaving the dead air to hang for Simon to fill.

"He's not going to sell you what you're looking for," a girl said from behind a stack of old magazines and books that Simon hadn't noticed. "The last guy who came in here asking for that kind of stuff cleaned him out already."

"What the hell are you doing back there?" the shop owner yelled. "I told you, you're not allowed in here."

The girl wore a dark blue sweatshirt, the hood pulled over her chin-length black hair. Her eyes were intense, especially since she looked like she was trying to psychically burn a hole through the shop owner's head. While her eyes exuded confidence, her posture told Simon she didn't feel 100 percent comfortable in her own skin. The confrontation was a struggle for her.

"I'm serious, young lady. If you're not out of my shop in two seconds, I'm calling the cops," the owner said.

"Call the cops. Maybe they'll be interested to hear all about the illegal metahuman items you've been selling out of here without a license," the girl replied.

The man retreated to the back of the store, presumably to make good on his promise to call the police. Neither the girl nor Simon seemed worried about this threat. Simon took a couple of steps in the girl's direction, careful not to seem overeager, even though he was eager for more information now that the pawnshop was looking like a dead end.

"So, I'm not in the wrong place, huh?" Simon asked the girl.

"You're not, but you're also barking up the wrong tree if you think I can help you get whatever you're after."

"What if I told you all I'm after is a little information?"

"I'd tell you I still can't help you."

"And what if I made it worth your while?"

"Depends on how much you think my while is worth."

All at once, the lights turned off, leaving Simon and the girl in the dark. The streetlights outside offered only a sliver of illumination.

"That probably means we should leave," the girl suggested.

"You don't seem like the type to give up so easily," he replied.

"I'm not, but the lights usually go off right before he lowers the security gate out front. I thought he'd learned his lesson the last time he locked me in her for the night and I trashed the place, but I guess not."

Simon glanced around at the messy shop. "This place can get worse?"

"I'm not sure he even noticed now that I think about it. Well, either way, I'm not looking to spend the night locked in a pawnshop. It's a free country, so you do whatever you want, but I'm leaving."

As if on cue, the motorized front gate whirred into action and slowly descended in front of the shop's window. Simon and the girl left through the front door and ducked under the gate.

"What's your name?" Simon asked once they were out on the sidewalk.

"Amanda Khan. You?"

The completely legitimate question caught Simon off guard. It'd been quite some time since someone had asked him his name.

"Simon," he replied.

"Sounds completely made up, but whatever. Have a good night, Simon."

Amanda turned on her heels to leave.

"Hey, wait a minute," Simon called after her. "What about that information?"

"Eh, not worth the trouble. Having a pair of old meta-bands you can mount above your fireplace and impress your other rich friends with isn't worth the trouble of dealing with the types of people who move that stuff around. Trust me."

"How do you know I'm rich?" Simon asked, intrigued by Amanda's intuition.

"You found this place, which tells me you've done enough homework to know that meta artifacts don't come cheap. When you tried to bribe me, you didn't offer a dollar amount. That tells me you're not only used to bribing people and getting your way, but also that the amount of money it'd take to get me to tell you what could be useless information isn't important to you. Also, your clothes and shoes are all brand new."

She'd barely turned around to deliver her answer before continuing to walk away. Amanda didn't wait for Simon's response to see whether she was right. She knew she was.

Simon was astounded at how quickly and succinctly Amanda had gotten a read on him, even if he wasn't necessarily *rich* the way she assumed. He was embarrassed that he'd made the rookie mistake of wearing clothes he hadn't worn in, but he hadn't had time and didn't think it would cause him to stand out as much as it did.

His leads had gone dry, but maybe this girl would be able to provide a couple of new ones.

THREE

Amanda was running out of ideas. What she wasn't short on was time, so she decided to stake out the pawnshop's back door. The shop owner knew more than he was willing to tell her. She could feel it. It was unlikely he could have closed the gate remotely or left *that* quickly, so odds were he was still inside the shop, waiting for the coast to clear before making a beeline for the exit. If that was the case, then Amanda would be out back waiting for him.

"You looking for someone?" a voice asked out of the darkness.

"I already told you I'm not interested in helping you find new items for your trophy case, buddy," she replied to the figure she assumed was the weirdo from the pawnshop as he approached her from the alley.

"I don't got a trophy case, but maybe I should think about it. What would you think about being the first thing I put in it?"

This wasn't the same person she had spoken with in the shop, but the realization came too late. This new person was standing between her and the easiest way out of the alley.

"Just beat it, all right?" She'd meant it to sound like a command rather than a question, but Amanda couldn't help it. She was scared.

"You just seem to be asking an awful lot of questions in places where you shouldn't be asking them."

Another man had snuck up behind her through the alleyway leading to the street without her noticing, and he wasn't alone. In seconds, she found herself surrounded. She glanced up at the security camera perched above the pawnshop's back door, wondering if it offered help or if the shop owner was on the other end, watching with a smile on his face.

"The old man isn't gonna help you. How do you think we heard about you being back here and asking questions?"

"Okay, got it. I'll stop asking questions. Message received, okay?"

None of the three men answered her. The closest thing to a response she got were their menacing grins.

She'd only have one good chance to make a break for it before all decorum went out the window. She took a deep breath as discreetly as possible and glanced past the men, feigning that she saw something unusual. Only one took the bait and turned to see what was behind him. It wasn't much of a break, but it was all she was going to get, so Amanda ran for the narrow alley.

She made it a few feet before a hand grabbed her by the hair and pushed her into the nearby dumpster. The other two closed in, taking advantage of the dumpster to pen her in. She was trapped.

"You told the old man that you understood last time, but here we are, so it would seem that the message *wasn't* received," the leader of the group growled at her. "That's why this time we're gonna give you a message you won't misunderstand."

The three men's heads all slammed together with such force that the sound caused her to jump. The men fell in a heap, piled on top of each other, knocked out cold. That's when Amanda saw their attacker standing behind them, wiping his hands as calmly as if he'd just taken the trash out to the curb.

"Go back out to the sidewalk, find a payphone, call the police," he told her. "Don't worry. These guys aren't going anywhere for a while."

Simon turned and walked down the alley, farther from the street and deeper into the darkness. Amanda's brain was still trying to process what had just unfolded. Her flight or fight response was confused now that neither was necessary.

She looked down at the men again. One of them was snoring; otherwise, Amanda would have wondered if they were dead, considering how quickly and violently Simon had rendered them unconscious. When she glanced back up, Simon was already difficult to see at the opposite end of the alleyway.

Amanda prided herself on not looking a gift horse in the mouth and knew she should just count herself lucky, head back to the street, and call 911. Maybe it was the adrenaline her body had released in a panic when she thought the men were about to assault her, but before she could internalize the decision, she was sprinting down the alley to catch up with Simon.

"You're not very good at following directions," he told her without breaking his stride or turning to face her.

"Neither are you. I told you I wasn't interested in giving

you information, but you obviously followed me anyway," she replied.

"Which you're welcome for, by the way."

"I could have handled myself back there."

"No, you couldn't have."

"Umm, yes, I could have. I took self-defense classes last summer. I could have put those guys down anytime I wanted."

"Well, you sure seemed to be waiting for the perfect time."

"You were watching me?"

"Yes, and trust me, I wouldn't have stepped in unless you'd needed me to. This was the last thing I needed today."

The pair walked a few paces in silence. Amanda trailed behind by a step or two despite her attempts to catch up and match his stride. The adrenaline was easing out of her system now that she didn't need it. She felt like she needed to puke, but she would settle for just sitting down for a minute to catch her breath.

"Can we stop for a minute?" she asked.

"You can do whatever you like. In fact, I'd appreciate it if you did."

"Two minutes ago you wouldn't leave me alone, and now you're practically running away from me."

"Not running away from you. Putting distance between me and the crime scene I created before the police arrive to ask questions."

"Speaking of which, how exactly did you do that?" Amanda asked, gesturing toward the unconscious would-be assailants.

Simon said nothing.

Amanda continued behind him. They turned onto the street, and his pace slowed to a more reasonable clip. There was no need to draw any attention, and that's just what walking in a hurry would do if he wasn't careful.

"I can help you, you know," Amanda offered, breaking the silence. Still no response. "That stuff you're looking for, I know who bought it."

He stopped dead in his tracks, which caused Amanda to run right into his back. He turned but said nothing, only offering to listen.

"I know who bought the stuff you're looking for," she repeated.

"You don't even know what I'm looking for," he replied.

"Doesn't matter what you're looking for. If it has anything to do with metahumans, I know who bought it."

FOUR

"This is the place," Simon told Amanda.

"Um, you live here?" she asked.

Simon didn't answer as he fished the key out of his pants pocket and jammed it into the padlock attached to a chain wrapped around a set of double doors. His gloved hands fumbled with the lock for a few seconds. He wasn't accustomed to entering through the front door, but it would raise less suspicion if anyone happened to be watching. Not like anyone would be, considering where they were.

"Whoa, does that sign still work?" Amanda asked as she pointed up to it.

The building was windowless from the outside, with only a broken neon sign marking the entryway. There was too much damage to tell what it had originally read. Otherwise, the building was completely nondescript.

"It's irrelevant."

"Maybe to you, but I still haven't decided if I'll tell you everything I know yet."

Simon stopped fiddling with the padlock and glared at

Amanda. He was already taking a gigantic risk in bringing her here and wasn't in the mood for games. He gave the stuck key one last hard turn, and the rust gave way enough for the padlock to disengage. Simon used another key on the same keychain to unlock the front door before opening it. The interior was pitch black.

"After you," he said.

Simon noticed Amanda hesitate for a moment as she likely thought about how insanely dangerous it was to follow a strange man into a darkened building. Despite this, she stepped into the darkness. Her eyes were searching for an exit when the metal door slammed shut behind her. If the building was dark before, now it was like floating in outer space.

After three long seconds in total darkness, her breathing quickened. Then the door's lock clicked shut.

Simon flipped a few switches, and the familiar hum of electricity filled the surrounding space. Amanda let out of a sigh of relief that at least this crazy guy hadn't just locked her in there and run away. He was in here too.

Then light started filling the room. Not all at once, and not so much as to subtract from the overall darkness of the space. The space revealed itself.

"You live in a video arcade?" she practically squealed.

Simon nodded and finished flicking a few remaining switches and levers before closing the breaker panel on the wall. Amanda briskly walked around the room, taking in the rows upon rows of stand-up cabinets that stretched endlessly in every direction. She ran her hand over the controls of the games that were familiar to her from her childhood, along with a few that just looked interesting.

Simon brushed past her and headed deeper into the building.

"Don't get me wrong, I would love to live in an arcade. It would be my dream to live in an arcade. But, um, why do you live in an arcade?" she asked.

Without being asked, Amanda followed.

"I'm pretty sure you have information to give me. That was our agreement, was it not?" Simon said without looking back, confident that she was following him.

He found his way to a skinny metal spiral staircase and rapidly ascended it. Amanda couldn't believe the distance he'd put between them in a matter of seconds, but in her defense, she'd never climbed a spiral staircase before and she was taking in the view of the dusty arcade cabinets as she made her way to the second floor, nearly twenty feet up. A tiny landing led to a door that Simon had already opened and disappeared through.

There was barely enough room for both of them to fit inside the office that had belonged to the arcade's owner back in its heyday. Simon pushed out the rolling chair; that, along with a desk, computer, and security camera monitors, took up 75% of the small space. He sat on the desk and gestured for Amanda to take the office chair.

"Aren't you going to take your gloves off?" Amanda asked.

Simon ignored her. He always kept his gloves on. Old habit.

"So, who's buying metahuman-related items from the pawnshop?" he asked.

"His name is Neil Guest," she said.

When it became clear she wouldn't elaborate, Simon said, "Okay, well, I'm going to need a little more information than that."

"So, why an arcade?"

"Rent was cheap. Neil Guest," he said, attempting to get Amanda back on track.

"Rent's cheap in a lot of places around here. Why an arcade, though?"

She was referring to the part of town they were in, Leighsville. The fallout from The Battle had hit the area hard. Any building taller than a few stories had been sliced in half by a laser beam projected from a metahuman Jones had bear-hugged into putty. A year later, this part of the city was still a ghost town, with few investors willing to put forth the funds to clean up the debris still piled on some corners.

Simon sighed and realized quid pro quo would be the quickest way to get the information he needed out of Amanda.

"The building is one of the few in the city that is set up for massive power needs, as necessitated by the arcade machines."

"Hmm, why do you need so much power?"

"Nope, it's my turn to ask a question. Who is Neil Guest?"

"He's this scumbag my idiot friend Lily thought she was in love with."

"How is that related to metahuman relics?"

Amanda sighed and looked down at her hands, which were fidgeting with the drawstrings of her hoodie. "If I tell you something, will you use it against me?"

"Depends on what it is," Simon said without hesitation.

Amanda was taken aback, not having expected such a frank response. "Well, that certainly makes me feel comfortable opening up."

Simon didn't respond or change his posture or expression. She wanted to tell him what she'd referred to; otherwise, she never would have brought it up.

"Me and Lily were both metahumans," she finally said, her eyes closed to avoid eye contact.

When Simon didn't respond, she pried one eye open to take in Simon's reaction. He remained stoic.

"You're not going to react to that?" The question was half surprise, half apology.

"I'm still waiting to hear something interesting," he said, knowing this would tick her off and open the door for more information to come tumbling out of her.

"Something interesting? I just told you I was a superhuman, that I had a pair of magical bracelets that gave me powers, and you're going to sit there and say, 'Tell me something interesting'? Are you for real?"

"The metabands aren't magic," Simon said.

"How the hell would you know? Last I checked, I didn't see you at any metahuman meetings," she said sarcastically.

"Last I checked, there weren't any heroes around Empire City that matched your description."

"I never said I was a hero."

"Well, now we have something interesting, don't we?"

Amanda had revealed more than she'd wanted to on the subject, but she was in too deep to turn back now.

"I wasn't a bad guy either, if that's what you're thinking. Neither was Lily. We just weren't into all the dressing up in Halloween costumes and giving ourselves dopey-sounding names bullshit. Our ... powers, or whatever you call them, were complimentary. Do you know what that means?"

Simon nodded.

"She could turn into like a gas or vapor or something. Just out of nowhere, poof, she could go from being a completely solid, normal human being into, like, a cloud."

"And what about you?"

"I could control the air. Not really the air, I guess, but more like the wind. I could move air around me in any direction I wanted to with my mind. As you might have already guessed, neither of our powers was especially dazzling. But together? Together they became very interesting."

"How so?" Simon asked, even though some possibilities were already evident to him.

"There wasn't a security system on earth we couldn't bypass. Bars, alarms, laser beams, it didn't matter. As long as there was a way to get air in from the outside, breaking in was a piece of cake. She'd cloud-up or whatever you want to call it, and I'd steer her through whatever air vent or heating duct we could find. I could get her in anywhere. Once she was in, she would become solid again, grab whatever we wanted, and then change back into air so I could pull her out. When she'd rematerialize, she'd have all the stolen loot she could fit in her arms."

"And how long did you two get away with this?"

"Once."

"Once?"

"We found our metabands only a few days before The Battle ended everything. We barely had a chance to use them before they all stopped working. But Lily was obsessed."

"Obsessed with what?"

"With the power, duh. She said she'd never felt the kind of freedom the metabands gave her. When they all stopped working, she took it pretty hard. Started hanging around with some unsavory characters, including Neil Guest."

"Was Neil her boyfriend?"

"Something like that."

"Why would Neil be buying metahuman relics from the pawnshop?"

"If I knew that, I'd be following that lead instead of waiting outside a pawnshop night and day for clues. Until you came along today, I felt like I was losing my mind staking that place out for so long."

"Do you know where I can find Neil?"

"I have an idea."

FIVE

Amanda told Simon all she knew, which wasn't much. Lily had gone to the pawnshop to trade her powerless metabands for cash. She'd stashed them in a box under her bed after losing hope they would ever function again after The Battle.

The man at the pawnshop offered to pass her information on to Neil. He described him as a collector who would be willing to offer her a nice price for the bands. Lily was confused as to why the man wouldn't just buy them from her and sell them to Neil himself, but he explained he would receive a nice finder's fee if Lily sold her bands.

She told Amanda everything, hoping she would offer to accompany her to the trade. Going to a pawnshop on her own was one thing, but meeting some sketchy guy that a pawnshop owner had referred her to? That was best done with a trusted third party present.

But Amanda was not happy. When Lily told her she was selling her metabands, Amanda couldn't understand why. In her mind, the metabands could wake back up at any moment. If Lily sold hers, she would regret it her entire life.

But deep down, Amanda's primary concern was what would happen if the metabands started working again and she was the only one of the two who had held on to theirs. The team would be done. It would just be Amanda by herself.

Instead of carefully articulating her concern to Lily, she got angry. She told Lily she didn't care, that she should sell her metabands, that she didn't want to be partners with her again, even if they started working.

Lily was hurt. She'd been struggling with the decision to sell her metabands and had only arrived at the idea when she felt like she had no other choice. She was young and had a criminal record. Finding a job had been difficult before The Battle, but with the city's economy in free fall, it felt all but impossible. She'd come to Amanda thinking she of all people would understand and be supportive. She even thought that maybe Amanda would want to sell her metabands too. It wasn't like Amanda was flush with cash either.

But when Lily suggested this, Amanda flew off the handle even harder. She told Lily she would never sell her metabands even if she was out on the streets.

Upset, Lily told Amanda she was going to meet with Neil and sell her bands without her. Hoping she was bluffing, Amanda told her to leave. She waited for hours for Lily to return. She thought Lily would come back and tell her she'd been right all along. That it was a scam or that the guy never showed. She'd hoped Lily would think about all the things Amanda had said and change her mind. But she didn't.

When Amanda hadn't heard from Lily by the next day, she started to worry. They'd never gone so long without speaking. She debated calling Lily all afternoon before finally caving in.

"Calling to apologize?" Lily asked.

She was relieved Lily was alive and presumably unharmed, but the question threw her. In her mind, Lily was the one who was supposed to be apologizing.

"Why should I apologize?" Amanda said. "I was just calling to make sure that guy didn't chop you up into pieces and throw you into a river somewhere."

"Nope, sorry. Actually, Neil's really great. He wasn't sketchy at all. You wouldn't believe how much he paid me for my metabands. I even told him it was too much, but he insisted. I'm meeting up with him later tonight. He wants me to come to a meeting."

"A meeting? What is this, alcoholics anonymous?"

"No, it's a meeting at the organization he works for."

"What organization?"

"He works for The Receptive."

Amanda had heard of The Receptive before, but she didn't know the details. They struck her as weird, preachy metahuman worshippers. She was surprised they'd invited Lily to a meeting. Amanda thought they didn't exist anymore. The organization revolved around metahumans, so what good were they now, with the metahumans all gone?

"AND THAT'S all you know about Neil? That he works for The Receptive?" Simon asked Amanda.

"More or less. That was the last time me and Lily spoke. I heard a few things from people about Neil after that, but I've never seen him in person myself. That's why I was hanging out at that pawnshop. I was hoping he'd show up again to talk with the owner. It's not much, but it's the only lead I have to go on to find Lily."

"Did you ever try to speak with him at their offices?"

"The Receptive? Yeah. I went there and asked for him, but they wanted to know who I was and what I wanted before they got him. The receptionist called security when I refused. They told me I wasn't allowed back there."

"And you listened to them?"

"Of course not, but their security is good. I can't make it more than a few steps into the lobby before they throw my ass back out of there."

"Hmm."

"Hmm? What are you *hmming* about?"

"Security. They're a quasi-religious organization. Having full-time security on site seems like overkill."

Simon gestured for Amanda to get up from the seat. She sighed and stood. Simon then swiveled the seat around to face the computer sitting on the desk and booted it up. Amanda was surprised that he was using such an old machine. It looked like it couldn't even connect to the internet, but the operating system looked surprisingly modern. She glanced underneath the desk to see if the old monitor wasn't plugged into a more modern machine.

"The Receptive has been mostly quiet since metabands stopped working," Simon said. "Their membership has been declining."

"Well, duh. Wasn't their whole thing promising any idiot who would listen a pair of shiny new metabands if they just believed hard enough?"

This was an oversimplification, but mostly true. Making promises was how they'd grown out of nowhere fast, and it explained how they'd dropped off the map just as rapidly.

A man named Alastair Green started the organization.

Not much was known about Green before he found his pair of metabands. Rumor had it that he'd been a preacher in his previous life. Other rumors stated he'd been a con artist who ripped off little old ladies by selling them reverse mortgages they didn't understand. The truth was likely somewhere in between.

Amanda was reluctant to give Simon Neil's location without a promise that she could accompany him, but he could procure the address himself with a quick internet search.

"You still need me there. I've been there before. I know the layout of the place," Amanda reasoned.

"No."

"He won't talk to you, you know. They'll just turn you away at the front desk."

Simon didn't respond verbally, but he seemed to understand that he'd need help to get past the front desk. He walked around the chair Amanda was sitting in and unlocked a drawer under the desk. He swiftly pulled out a pair of metabands and placed them into a duffle bag.

"Whoa! Are those actually—" Amanda began before Simon cut her off.

"It doesn't matter. They're not leaving my possession. But they'll be enough to get me through the front door if this Neil is as desperate for metabands as you say." Simon swung the duffle bag strap over his shoulder. "I'll be back in two hours."

"You can't just lock me in here."

"Who said anything about locking you in here? You're free to leave whenever you want."

"Great, I'm out of here, then," Amanda said reflexively, embarrassed by Simon's declaration that she didn't have to stay.

"Be careful. Once word gets back to whoever sent those guys after you, they'll likely start looking for you again."

"Whatever."

"Don't worry about locking up after you leave," Simon said as he walked out the door.

SIX

"Hi there. Welcome to The Receptive Center, Empire City. How may I assist you today?" the receptionist asked Simon with a smile plastered on her face. She wore a pale pink dress, and her blonde hair was pulled back in a tight bun. Her lipstick and nails were a matching shade of bright red. Simon guessed she was in her early twenties, but her manicured and professional appearance made her seem older.

The center almost never closed their doors, a fact that benefitted Simon who still preferred to work at night whenever possible.

He did his best to return a courteous smile, placing it on his face like a mask. "Hi, my name is Simon. I'm looking for Neil Guest. I was told I could find him here?"

Simon didn't use an alias since it was possible Neil was already aware of his efforts to locate metahuman artifacts. It was a long shot, but if Neil was already aware of him, then using a different name would set off alarm bells. Better to be safe than sorry.

"Umm, I'm not sure we have anyone here by that name.

May I ask what this is regarding?" the receptionist asked, her smile wavering.

Simon had anticipated the question. He placed the duffle bag on the reception desk and unzipped it. Before he even fully unzipped the bag, the reflection from the meta-bands inside caught the receptionist's eye, and she rose to her feet in a panic. Without asking, she grabbed the zipper from Simon's grip and closed the bag back up.

"Oh! You're here to see Neil. I must have misheard you. I do apologize. Please, have a seat and I'll see if he's in."

She directed Simon to a chair in the small empty lobby. As he sat down, he saw that the receptionist was already on the phone.

"No. Yes. He just started taking them out of a bag..." Simon couldn't hear the receptionist, but he could read her lips as she talked into the phone in hushed tones. She was nervous, but she'd known who to call about this unexpected visitor. "Of course," she said before hanging up and rising to her feet. She walked around the desk and over to Simon. "Mister...?"

"Just Simon is fine."

"Of course. Simon, if you could follow me, I'll bring you to a more private room for you to wait."

Simon followed the receptionist past the desk and through a door that required her badge to open. Beyond the door was a hallway with rooms on either side. The doors to each room were closed. On each was a single digit number in numerical order, but no other markings indicated the purpose of each room or what lay behind the door. Simon glanced at the gap under the doors and saw a sliver of light, suggesting the rooms were occupied. The receptionist stopped at Room 7 and swiped her badge over the magnetic reader mounted on the wall. The lock clicked softly, and she opened the door, motioning for Simon to enter first.

"Quite the security system you have here," he remarked upon passing her.

"An unavoidable necessity nowadays, unfortunately."

"What does that mean?"

"There are a lot of nuts out there. You may have a seat. Neil will be with you in a few minutes."

The receptionist glanced at the duffle bag in Simon's hand before exiting the room. He heard the lock reengage when the door closed and wondered if he could exit the room. There was another badge reader on the wall inside the room, meaning it was very possible he was locked inside. He wasn't concerned, though—not yet.

Simon took one of the two chairs in the room, each facing the other across a simple table. The similarity to a police interrogation room wasn't lost on him. The room was blank besides the sparse furniture and the television mounted on the wall, which displayed The Receptive logo lazily bouncing around the screen to prevent burn-in. Simon sighed, wondering how long he would be stuck waiting in the room, when the television screen changed.

It began playing a video of beautiful landscapes from around the world, set to relaxing music. A narrator began speaking. Simon wondered if they were playing the video to recruit him or if the room was set up to play it on a loop. Either way, he was interested in what information the video contained, although for different reasons from The Receptive.

"Hello, and welcome to The Receptive Center, Empire City. You've taken an important first step in helping to unlock not only your full potential, but the potential of the entire human race.

"Unlike some elements of society, The Receptive recognizes the power that has been given to metahumans all around the world and the responsibility they have to share that power with the human race. We're creating a brighter future than anyone ever imagined possible, and it all starts with you."

A small beep sounded on the other side of the door, followed by the lock disengaging. The door opened, and a well-dressed young man entered. Simon guessed he was in his mid-twenties. He wore an off-the-rack suit not tailored to his slender frame. His blond hair was short and sharp, as was the glint in his eye as he extended his hand for Simon to shake.

"Neil Guest. And you must be...?"

"Simon."

"No last name, Simon?" Neil asked, laughing with too much vigor at what wasn't a joke.

"Just Simon is fine for now, I think."

"Okay. All right. Right down to business. I can appreciate that." Neil held the door open and gestured for Simon to follow him. "I think we'd be more comfortable speaking in my office. That way, we can be sure we won't be interrupted."

Simon rose from his seat and followed Neil down the hallway to Room 3. He swiped his badge across the reader and opened the door for Simon to enter.

Neil's office was more personalized than the sterile room Simon had waited in. Wood paneling covered the walls to warm up the space. It didn't completely work, but it was still an upgrade from the other spaces Simon had seen so far in the building.

Along the walls were various plaques and certificates, with The Receptive logo featured. There were certificates for passing vaguely named courses and awards for outstanding achievements in such broad topics as "Humanity" and "Openness." There were also several photographs of Neil alongside Alastair Green. Some were posed, but others were candid photos of the pair on stage together or Neil looking on while Alastair spoke with world leaders and celebrities.

"This is quite the display you have here," Simon said.

Neil closed the door and took the chair behind his mahogany desk that was far too large for the room. He hadn't yet offered Simon a chair, choosing to let him pace around the room, admiring his awards.

"Thank you. Of course, you never work with the sole purpose of garnering nice awards to hang around your office, but the recognition is still very nice."

"You must have been with the organization for quite some time."

"Yes. My parents joined when I was quite young, so I was lucky to learn the teachings of The Receptive during a formative time in my life."

"They must be proud of you."

There was a brief hesitation.

"Yes, they are," Neil said.

The hesitation before he answered told Simon his parents were either deceased or estranged from Neil. He guessed the latter based on Neil's use of the present tense.

"I'm sure this past year has taken its toll on your organization," Simon said.

Neil looked genuinely confused by the change in topic.

"I just mean with all the metahumans being gone and all," Simon explained.

"Oh, because of the reset?" Neil asked.

"Reset?"

"You're referring to the temporary deactivations. The metabands. We refer to it as a reset."

"I'm not sure I follow."

"Well, Mr. Simon, we believe a higher power is responsible for the temporary deactivation of metabands. The same higher power that bestowed them upon Earth in the first place. We've misused them to tragic consequences, and much like a toddler who has misbehaved, the human race has been placed into a 'time out' of sorts until we can use the power that comes with metabands responsibly. Use them to improve the conditions of all those around the world rather than using them to see who can punch the hardest."

"So, you don't think the metabands are off for good?"

"Oh, heaven's no! There's nothing to indicate that's the case."

"There's nothing to indicate it isn't either. We know as much about them now as we ever have."

"That's where you're wrong, Mr. Simon. While the public may not know much about metabands, how they work, etcetera, we've been blessed with the teachings of Alastair Green, a man who understands metabands at their fundamental level. As a civilization, we're incredibly lucky that the one man who understands how metabands work has decided to share that knowledge with anyone willing to open their eyes and heart to the truth. It's truly a beautiful sentiment, and one we believe will result in metabands around the world reactivating once the truth has spread to everyone."

Simon could see in his eyes that Neil was a true believer.

"Well then, that certainly goes a long way in explaining

why you might be interested in the item I have with me today," Simon said.

"Ah, yes, of course. I apologize. Sometimes I get so caught up in the true message we are trying to disseminate to people that all other concerns are pushed aside. Would you care to show me what it is you've brought today?"

"Of course," Simon said. as he reached for the duffle bag lying at his feet. He unzipped the top and pulled the two metabands out, offering them to Neil for closer inspection.

Neil took one of the metabands into his hand and ran his fingers across the surface—first the outer, then the inner, back and forth, paying close attention.

"Where did you find these?" he asked.

"I found them in the trash."

"So, they did not belong to you?"

"I wish. No, I found them a few weeks ago. I suppose whoever they belonged to had no use for them anymore."

"Fascinating. Well, I have to tell you what you have here are in fact genuine."

"You can tell that even though they don't work anymore?"

"Yes. When you've spent as much time with these as I have, you learn the subtle tactile qualities of the elements used to craft them. They're impossible to replicate with any techniques known to man, so once you are aware of them, forgeries become quite blatant. No, Mr. Simon, what you have here is the genuine article."

"Does that mean they're worth money?"

"They're worth something far more valuable than money, Mr. Simon. What if I told you that one day soon these metabands might work again?"

"You're saying I could use them to become a metahuman?"

"I'm saying, if you're interested, there is an opportunity for you to learn the teachings we offer here."

"Oh. I don't think I'm interested in joining a new religion. No offense to you, of course."

"The Receptive isn't a religion any more than any other branch of science is. We are studying and putting into practice discoveries we make about metabands and metahumans that the outside world has yet to comprehend."

"Like what?"

Neil laughed. "I'm sorry, Mr. Simon. While we believe in transparency, there are elements of our discoveries that the outside world is not ready to learn about. We only share those discoveries with other members, but they are something you could share in if you chose to explore the path to becoming a Receptive yourself."

"Hmm, I'm not really sure. I was kinda just looking to turn these around and make a few bucks."

"Well, that's certainly something we can discuss as well, but I do want you to think about it. Has it ever occurred to you that you found these metabands for a reason?"

"In the trash?"

"Especially in the trash. Another few hours and these would have been carted off to a landfill and buried under a pile of trash. Perhaps another living soul wouldn't have found them for hundreds of thousands of years, if ever. But then you came along, and something about these metabands called out to you. Something told you to look where they were. Don't you find that extraordinary?"

"I never really thought about it that way."

Just then, a phone on top of Neil's desk rang with a peculiar, urgent tone.

"I'm so sorry, but I have to take this," Neil said. He answered the phone without saying a word and sat silently

before returning the receiver to its cradle. "I beg your fore-
giveness, but I must ask you to excuse me for just a moment.
We seem to be having a somewhat urgent situation downstairs that I need to tend to, but please, make yourself
comfortable while I'm gone and I'll return as quickly as
possible."

Simon had intended to respond to this, but before he
could open his mouth, Neil was out the door. He could hear
Neil's footsteps echoing down the hall as he broke into a
run. Whatever was happening downstairs that required his
attention was indeed urgent.

Simon didn't waste a single second jumping into the
chair Neil had vacated. He'd made the mistake of leaving an
adept computer expert in his office alone. Simon didn't
expect to encounter many safeguards on Neil's desktop
computer since it sat behind a series of locked doors, and he
was happy to see he was correct. Within seconds, after
exploiting a series of backdoors, Simon was logged into
Neil's account.

On the desktop was the icon for a common commercial
security camera solution. Double-clicking it brought up a
dozen cameras that monitored rooms throughout the building. Two of them showed different angles of the lobby. It
was still empty, except for its new occupant: Amanda Khan.

There was no audio from the security feed, but Simon
didn't need any. Whatever Amanda was saying wasn't as
important as the way she was saying it: loudly. She was
screaming at the receptionist and pounding her hand on the
desk. A security officer entered the scene, and Amanda took
a handful of pamphlets left on the lobby table, tore them up,
and threw them in the air. Even though Amanda was half
the size of the security guard, Simon could see the terror in
his eyes.

Simon knew he didn't have much time before Neil returned, so he quickly navigated to a File Manager window and clicked through the hierarchy of folders for anything interesting. Within the recent documents folder, he found a folder marked "Fort Grey."

Opening the folder, Simon discovered dozens of thumbnails of blueprints and schematics. He jammed a small thumb drive into the USB port and began copying them over, only to discover the files were too large to transfer in the limited time he had.

He changed windows to check on the commotion in the lobby. Neil was in front of Amanda. She appeared calmer than before, but she was still shouting. She must have agreed to leave calmly if Neil came out to see her. Something about Amanda frightened Neil. Most people would have called the police to have Amanda removed. Neil hadn't, though. He was willing to humor Amanda to a certain degree and didn't want the cops involved. He was guilty of more than he let on.

The computer was still working to open the enormous image files into the photo viewing software. The first image opened and showed only plumbing plans for a large facility. There was no further information to glean, but it was unusual enough for Simon to keep digging. If Green and his people were building a compound, Simon wanted to know where.

A few subfolders down he found the jackpot: a spreadsheet detailing the group's holdings of massive amounts of land within the state. Simon had heard that Alastair claimed to choose what land to purchase based on what his metabands told him.

The purchases were complex, likely a means of cooking his books to make it easier for him to skim from the top. The purchases always happened through shell corporations and often closed for above market price. Some even appeared to be straight up donations from followers to the organization.

Together, the files showed that The Receptive owned thousands upon thousands of acres, and much of it was wilderness—the perfect place to build a compound off the grid.

Simon clicked back to the security camera feed. Neil was on the reception desk phone, and Amanda was retreating through the front doors. He must have called Amanda's bluff by phoning the police, or he was pretending to.

Right before she turned and pushed her way out the front door, she glanced up at the security camera. That's when Simon knew for sure that Amanda had created a diversion for him. It hadn't been part of the plan, but Amanda had been impressed enough with Simon to guess that he would put the few minutes alone in enemy territory to good use.

On the screen, Neil watched Amanda walk out the door and then hung up the phone when he was confident she wouldn't try to come back inside. He spoke to the receptionist, but his back was to the camera so Simon couldn't read his lips. Then he walked around the reception desk toward the locked door.

Simon cursed before closing all the open windows, removing the USB drive, and putting the computer back to sleep. He settled back into his chair seconds before Neil entered the room.

"I'm sorry about that," he said as he walked back to his chair.

"Is everything okay?" Simon asked, mimicking sincerity.

"Everything's fine. Just a troublemaker off the street."

"Does that happen here a lot?"

"I wish I could tell you it didn't, Simon, but unfortunately, many people in this world are afraid of the lessons we teach here. The way they see it, if they aren't happy with the way they see the world, then we shouldn't be either. We don't let them bother us, though. Actually, we feel sorry for them. We pray they'll soon see the errors of their ways and the way the world and metahumans are really supposed to be."

"Of course," Simon replied. Half the things coming out of Neil's mouth were mired in nonsense. Simon didn't see what else he could gain from the conversation and needed to remove himself from the situation.

"Simon, may I ask you a question?" Neil asked.

"Okay," Simon said, expecting another senseless diatribe.

"You don't know that girl who came in here, do you?"

"Excuse me?" Simon asked.

"The girl who was just in our lobby, you don't happen to know her, do you?" he asked again calmly.

"I'm not sure what you're talking about," Simon replied, squinting to sell his confusion.

"I suppose it doesn't matter," Neil said.

Simon assumed Neil knew he wouldn't reveal his knowing Amanda. The question had been meant to throw Simon off balance so Neil could sniff out whether this was a trap. It was time to make his exit.

"I can see the rumors about paranoia within your operation aren't without merit, Mr. Guest. I'll need some time to think about the future of these metabands. After all, I wouldn't want to be hasty and sell them cheap if they'll come back to life one day."

"Of course," Neil said through gritted teeth. "I wouldn't

want you to make a decision you'd later come to regret. I'm sure once you consider your other options you'll see we're by far the best course of action. I hope to welcome you again soon, maybe even as part of our congregation."

"Thank you, Mr. Guest," Simon said, ignoring Neil's suggestion.

SEVEN

"Any luck?" Amanda shouted as she walked through the front door to the arcade.

"Your little stunt back there wasn't cute," Simon answered from the upstairs office.

Hours had passed. It was late now, and Simon had wondered when Amanda would show up again.

Amanda closed the front door behind her and flipped the deadbolt. She walked up the metal spiral staircase to the manager's office. Inside, she found Simon seated at his computer.

"I don't care if it was cute if it gave you a chance to find some dirt."

"That's irrelevant because you just made all this much harder on me. Neil knows we're on to him, and that means he'll be watching us."

"You really need to update this thing," Amanda said, ignoring him. "You know they have these things called *flat screens* now. Get this, it's a screen, but it's flat. Not that I'm fat-shaming your monitor, but I think you're going blind trying to read off this screen."

"Are you even listening to me?" Simon asked.

"Sure. I think I can find out where the next Receptive seminar will be. I'm thinking we can both go undercover."

"They'll see through whatever your idea of a disguise is, and I wouldn't recommend you go."

"What do you mean?"

"Exactly what I said. I wouldn't recommend you go to the next seminar."

"You're not in charge of me, you know."

"I know I'm not. You're free to do whatever the hell you want. I'm doing you the favor of giving you my recommendation."

"And why would I take your advice? Don't get me wrong, you seem like you're a smart guy and all, but I'm failing to understand why your opinion on this matter is any better than mine."

"It just is. Listen, again, you can do whatever you like, but I'm telling you there's more to this. Alastair Green, Neil, this whole group—they're more organized than what you described. They're efficient. There's money coming in, a lot, and these people aren't fooling around. I'm not sure if they're dangerous, but they have the potential to be. They're focused on recruiting, and I'm certain they've figured out we know each other."

"So what?" Amanda said. "I can take care of myself."

"You've got to drop the tough-guy act."

"It's not an act!"

"Not everything is about brute force. You have to be smarter than this if you want answers about where your friend is. If you go back there tomorrow night, half the place will recognize you. Do you think getting answers will be easier when they have people keeping an eye on you? No. You'll be limiting your options over a wild stab in the dark."

"Well, not all of us have the luxury of being all Sherlock Holmes about everything. Some of us have people we care about and desperately want back, and we're willing to do whatever it takes to get them back."

Simon quickly lifted a single index finger to his lips.

"Don't tell me to be qui—" Amanda started, but Simon shot her a deadly look that shushed her without a word.

Then he cocked his head, listening.

Softly but swiftly, he moved out onto the small landing at the top of the staircase and peered where a metallic scraping noise was coming from. Through the front door window, he spotted two shadows that shouldn't have been there. A quick glance at the small security monitors on the desk confirmed his suspicions: someone, or more accurately, *five* someones were trying to break in.

Amanda saw them on the monitor and opened her mouth to ask Simon what was going on. He held up his hand again to silence her. A look of panic swept across her face. She was confused and not sure what to do.

Simon had helped her out, and she appreciated that. But what did she know about him? He seemed like he was on the same side as her, but it was too soon to be sure. She'd only come back here because she thought he could help her find her friend. She'd assumed he was a "good" guy, but what if he wasn't? What if these people were trying to break in because this guy owed them money? After all, who hid out in an abandoned arcade if they weren't hiding a secret from the rest of the world?

"Follow me," Simon told her and walked away before she acknowledged the instruction.

She froze, unsure if she should listen to him. Then she glanced back at the monitors and noticed that one of the men had a gun. He was hiding it from view while also shielding another man. The second man was crouched in front of the door, working on the lock.

Simon turned back when Amanda didn't follow.

"I'm not screwing around. Whoever they are, they're not here to play *Space Invaders*. If you come with me, I can keep you safe, but I can't do that if you stay up here."

Amanda's gut told her he was telling the truth, and her brain didn't have time to produce a counterargument. She nodded, and Simon began to descend the stairs, now with Amanda following closely behind. They reached the main floor and heard the sharp clang of a metal tool hitting the concrete floor outside the front door. It was followed by what sounded like a whispered argument.

"That door isn't reinforced and won't keep them out much longer," Simon whispered.

Is he going to try to take on these men? Amanda thought.

It was the most direct way to find out who they were and why they were here, but only if Simon could take them out quickly enough. Five against one were bad odds, though, especially when there were guns involved. If one man was armed, the other four were likely armed as well. On top of that, Simon had Amanda to worry about. No matter how quick Simon was, a stray bullet would always be quicker. He couldn't risk a close-quarters fight involving weapons when there was an innocent bystander involved.

Simon was backed into a corner. For him, there was always a way out, but sometimes that created more complications. This time there was only one option, and that option meant revealing the truth about who he really was to Amanda.

He motioned for Amanda to keep her head down and follow him. She listened and crouched, deciding to put all future decisions in his hands until she was safe.

It wasn't like she had a better option.

The pair wove in and out of different aisles. Amanda was completely turned around, but Simon knew exactly where he was heading. The arcade was dark. Not much was installed in the way of lighting since the machines provided more than enough ambient light when they were powered up.

The sound of wood cracking and the metal lock bouncing off the wooden floor broke the relative silence.

The men were inside.

"See, was that so hard?" one of the men said.

"Very discreet. I would have had the door open in another ten seconds if you'd let me finish instead of kicking it open," another man replied.

"We're in, aren't we?"

"We are, and now anyone who's in here knows it too, moron."

"There's nobody in here."

Amanda, her attention on where the men were talking, bumped into an arcade cabinet. The sound was quiet, but her gasp was not.

Suddenly, all the chatter between the men stopped.

They'd heard her.

Simon scrambled toward the end of the aisle. He was abandoning her, Amanda thought. He was cutting his losses and leaving her behind for the men to find. She considered making a run for it in the opposite direction from Simon, hoping if they found him, they might not bother looking for her.

But before she could decide, Simon reached the end of the aisle. He glanced up, clearly expecting Amanda to be right next to him. When he saw her at the other end of the aisle, he frowned and motioned for her to join him.

"There's a light on upstairs. Leonard, go check it out," one man said.

Amanda heard footsteps approaching and froze. She stayed perfectly still, crouched in the shadow of a *Ms. Pac-Man* machine. The man walked right in front of her, so close that Amanda could have reached out and grabbed him were she an idiot. If he had glanced to his left, he would have spotted her for sure. When she heard the clanging noise of boots ascending the metal spiral staircase, she turned and ran over to Simon as quickly and quietly as she could. When she reached him, he put a finger to his lips. Then he pushed on the coin slot of the arcade machine he was crouched in front of. The metal panel covering the front gave way and swung inward, revealing darkness inside. He motioned for Amanda to go in.

Hiding inside an empty arcade cabinet didn't seem like the noblest way to deal with this situation, but she wasn't about to wait around to find out what these guys wanted.

"Careful," Simon whispered as she crawled past him and into the empty space. She placed her left hand inside, moving on her knees, but when she went to put her right hand down, there was nothing beneath it. She nearly tumbled into the cabinet head over heels, but Simon grabbed onto her ankle to steady her. Amanda managed to keep from yelping, but just barely. Simon reached in and grabbed her right hand, guiding it onto a handhold.

This wasn't just an empty box in which to hide; it was an entrance.

Every time Amanda thought she'd reached the bottom of the ladder, she found another rung. She descended farther and farther in pitch-black darkness, securing her footing on the next rung before moving her hands. Only a faint light came in from above her, but since the arcade's main floor was dark, it did little to illuminate the tunnel.

The small shaft of light disappeared, and the arcade cabinet door clicked shut. A second later, she heard another pair of feet on the ladder, followed by the soft sound of the door sealing. Red emergency lighting flicked on, and Amanda pulled her body close to the ladder on instinct. Below her was a very long drop. It was hard for her to estimate just how long, but she wouldn't be walking away from a fall from this height if she lost her grip.

"You okay down there?" Simon asked from above.

She looked up and was surprised to find him only a few feet up. She was much closer to the entrance than she'd estimated, the darkness playing tricks with her mind.

"Don't worry," Simon said. "The second door is insulated against sound. Once it's closed, a bomb could go off outside and you wouldn't hear it."

"Oh, okay. I guess that explains everything, then," Amanda said.

Simon didn't appreciate the sarcasm, but he understood why she was angry and confused.

"Keep climbing. When we get to the bottom, I'll explain."

At the bottom of the ladder was a small concrete room with one door. That door had a window of mirrored glass. Amanda tried to peer through it anyway, but she only caught her reflection looking back at her.

Once Amanda was out of the way, Simon slid down the rest of the ladder, startling her.

"What is this place?" Amanda asked, barely able to get the words out.

He pressed his palm against a section of wall to the right

of the door that was a slightly lighter shade of gray than the rest of the concrete.

" Authorization code: 4923H1T."

The area of the wall glowed red around the outline of his hand. Inside the door, a heavy click sounded, like the pressure of a hydraulic piston release, and the locking mechanism in the door deactivated. The door swung easily on its hinge.

Simon took his hand off the wall and gently pushed the door open fully. "After you."

Dumbfounded, Amanda had to walk back into the smaller room to catch her breath and orient herself. What she saw was hard to believe.

In front of her was a space that stretched past the horizon. The ceiling was surprisingly low given the size of the space and how far underground they were. Much of the space was hidden in darkness, with lights positioned at random. There were strange-looking vehicles and workbenches alongside piles of rubble and machinery.

"It used to be a subway tunnel. The city shut down this line decades ago, though. After The Battle, the tunnel became inaccessible from both sides. It's abandoned, more or less."

"So, the way we came in is the only way in?"

"It's the easiest way in," Simon replied.

"And why would someone have an abandoned subway tunnel full of tools and equipment like fifty feet underneath an arcade?" Amanda asked.

"I haven't been completely truthful with you. I haven't lied, and I hope you'll realize the difference. With what I do, or *did*, it's a lot easier to keep things close to the vest until I have no other choice but to let someone in."

"Okay, sure ... That still doesn't explain what we're

doing in an abandoned subway tunnel, hiding from random dudes with guns."

"Before this, before all of this, before The Battle, I was someone else."

"Wait, you were a metahuman?"

"No, I wasn't. But I knew many of them. I was even lucky enough to call a few of them my friends."

Amanda's head spun as she put the pieces together. It all started to make sense: why he was looking for metahuman artifacts; how he could fight so well; why he lived in a rundown arcade in the middle of nowhere.

"We'll be safe down here," Simon said. He removed a large black tarp from a bank of computer monitors. Each screen lit up individually before booting, a few lines of code flashing on the screens. When the boot sequence was done, the monitors displayed various angles from the arcade above. Amanda hadn't noticed any security cameras inside the arcade, only outside, but judging by the monitors, the arcade was full of them.

Simon leaned over the desk in front of the monitors and punched commands into the workstation to isolate the faces of the men who'd broken in and run facial recognition algorithms against them.

"Hmm," he said.

"*Hmm* is what I was thinking too. Are you going to explain any of this?" Amanda asked.

"These men, I can't find a match in any of the country's criminal databases."

"Why do you have access to the country's criminal databases?"

"I have access because I took access. Added a few entries to the database myself over the years too. Quid pro quo."

Amanda moved to stand in the small gap between Simon and the monitors.

"Okay, enough. What the hell is going on here? What is all of this? Who the hell are you?" By the last question, she was shouting.

Simon could see her frustration had reached a boiling point and decided he needed to explain himself.

"So far, I've only told you what you needed to know for your protection and mine. It's obvious, though, that you've learned some of my secrets without the proper context. I'm sure entering a subterranean hideout without knowing why I have a subterranean hideout is confusing."

Amanda glared at him. "Understatement of the century."

"The person I am today isn't the person I was a year ago," he said.

"You mean The Battle?"

"Yes."

"So, wait. Were you in The Battle? I thought you said you weren't a metahuman?"

"I wasn't, but I was there. Before all this, I went by a different name. Midnight."

Amanda's eyes widened, and her jaw dropped. "Midnight? Like *Midnight* Midnight?"

Simon nodded.

"Holy sh—I just ... You're just some guy."

"Sorry to disappoint you."

"No, I'm not disappointed. It's just I never expected to meet you. Everyone said you died in The Battle. They all said that's why no one's ever seen you again."

"I survived, but I shouldn't have. I was teleported out of the city limits right as the heavy fighting started. By the time I got back, it was over and the metahumans were all gone."

"So, you just gave up?"

"No. I did everything I could to help."

"Then how come no one ever saw you with the mask on again?"

"When I got back to the city, the first damaged building I found was a hospital. Bystanders were already there, working to evacuate anyone who was still alive before the building collapsed. When I arrived wearing the mask, some ran. Others tried to keep me away. They thought I was a metahuman. The mask struck terror in them. Many were suffering from shock, understandably. I took the mask off that day to help. It hasn't felt right to put it back on."

On the monitors, the men were regrouping near the entrance. They hadn't found what they were looking for. When the last man returned from a final check of the upstairs office, the group exited through the front door.

Simon pushed back from the desk. "They must be connected to Alastair Green's group. They may have followed me back from The Receptive building. That would explain why I can't find them in any of the criminal databases: they aren't criminals. Or they're criminals who haven't been caught. It seems we've piqued someone's interest. Best to stay under the radar for a while."

"I thought we were already pretty far under the radar."

"I did too, or else I would never have risked coming back here. Maybe I'm just out of practice, but it's obvious we're dealing with a more serious situation than I anticipated."

Simon glanced back over at the monitors and tapped the one displaying a wide-angle shot of the street outside.

"Do you notice anything about that van?" he asked, pointing to a clean white van parked legally down the street from the arcade.

"Uh, not really. Looks like a normal van."

"It's too clean. We're in a rundown commercial neighborhood. Anyone driving a van around here has beat the thing to hell. That van looks like it just rolled off the lot. Also, the men who broke into the arcade all got into that van. They're staking this place out in case either of us shows up here."

"You think they know we're hiding in here?"

"They at least suspect we are. They definitely saw me enter. Otherwise, they wouldn't have broken in. Even if they don't know I'm still in here, they're waiting for me to come back. You're going to have to stay down here tonight, I'm afraid. There's a private room with a cot you can use."

"Umm, what about food? I'm starving and I was counting on hitting up a pizza parlor on my way home."

"You'll find protein bars and nutritional supplements in the cabinets down the hall."

"Mmm, nutritional supplements. Sounds delicious. So glad I waited to get that slice of pizza," Amanda said as she wandered down the hall toward the food.

Ignoring her sarcasm, Simon focused on the video image of the van.

AMANDA SPRANG AWAKE and jumped out of bed. It was so dark she couldn't even tell if her eyes were open or closed. Then she spotted a sliver of dull light, and everything came flooding back to her. She'd gorged herself on protein bars and then fallen soundly asleep. Adrenaline had kept her going, but once she was safe, her belly was full, and she was surrounded by darkness, she fell into a deep sleep.

She hadn't even taken her shoes off before climbing into the uncomfortable cot that had felt like a luxury king-sized mattress. Feeling her way through the darkness toward the sliver of light, she opened the door and stepped out into the hallway. Everything was the way she remembered it. Simon still sat at his workstation, staring at the security camera footage and other information that was too dense for her to decipher.

"I was wondering when you'd rejoin the land of the living," Simon said without turning to look at her. Whether some sensor on screen had alerted him to her waking up or he had heard her coming down the hallway, Amanda wasn't sure.

"How long was I out for?" she asked, rubbing the sleep from her eyes.

"Almost twelve hours," Simon answered.

"What?!" Amanda yelped in shock. "I slept through the entire night?"

"Technically, you slept through the entire day. It was almost morning by the time you went to bed."

"Why did you let me sleep so long?"

"You needed the rest. Your mind and body start playing tricks on you when you go too long without sleep."

"Did you get any sleep?"

"I don't need as much sleep as most people. Is there anyone you need to contact? You've been out of touch for a while, so if you need to let someone know you're okay, we can arrange that."

"No, it's fine," Amanda replied. Her tone implied she didn't want to discuss it further, and she quickly changed the subject. "What's the plan for us today?"

"There's no plan for us. I need to retrieve a tracking device I loaned to a friend."

"You have friends?"

Simon ignored the comment. He also conveniently left

out that the reason he needed to retrieve the tracking device was because he'd already planted his spare on Amanda's sweatshirt.

"I need you to stay here while I'm gone."

"You can't keep me here."

"You're right, but I don't have to help you find your friend either. If you want my help, we do this by my rules."

He'd felt a tinge of guilt planting the tracker on Amanda, but her defiance reassured him that it had been a smart idea. Simon got up from his chair and walked toward the entrance to the bunker.

"Don't wait up."

EIGHT

Simon stood alone in the ornate waiting area of a fancy restaurant. It had been a long time since he had found himself inside a restaurant. Mostly, he subsisted on things that either came in powder form or didn't require a stove.

The person he was waiting for had chosen the restaurant. It was called Nuovo Fiore and had a six-month-long wait list with a celebrity chef to match. He wore a black suit and black dress shirt that fit right in with the restaurant's vibe, which was lucky since the only suits he owned were black.

The door to the restaurant opened, and Simon's meeting strolled in. Her name was Aria Grey, but he knew her better as Luna. She wore a tight red dress that looked stunning on her. All eyes in the waiting area immediately turned to her. He wasn't thrilled that everyone was now staring at the person he was meeting, but he wasn't surprised.

"Well, well, well, you clean up nice after all. I always wondered whether that mask came off," Aria said to Simon.

Simon grimaced at the word "mask" and glanced at the

dozen or so people eavesdropping on the conversation between the beautiful woman in red and the man dressed in black.

"Here you go," Aria said as she handed Simon the tracking device he was after. Despite it being practically microscopic, he rushed to conceal it inside his jacket pocket.

The maître d' interrupted to inform them their table was ready. Grateful to be escaping the eyes of the lobby, Simon gestured for Aria to go ahead of him. They snaked their way through the crowded restaurant toward the secluded booth at the back corner of the dining room.

"You know I was kidding when I said this was where I wanted to meet, right?" Aria said. "Don't get me wrong, I'm thrilled to be here. The swordfish is supposed to be out of this world. I just suggested it as a joke because it's impossible to get a table. I should have known you'd not only get us in, but you'd also get us the best table."

Getting a reservation had been relatively easy. The computer system the restaurant used was hosted in-house without a firewall in sight. He felt bad canceling someone else's dinner reservations, but when he saw that the reservation was for a hedge fund manager under investigation for fraud, it eased some of his guilt.

The pair found their booth and were seated. The waiter filled their glasses and handed them each a wine list.

Aria collected the one in Simon's hands and returned both to the waiter. "We don't need these. We'll both have whiskeys neat, please. Whatever's the most expensive."

"Right away," the waiter said with a smile before leaving to fetch their drinks.

"Don't worry, I'm paying for tonight," Aria said.

"That's not what I'm worried about."

"You still drink whiskey neat, don't you? I can flag the waiter if you want to change your order."

"Whiskey is fine. I'm just curious how you can order off the menu in a place like this without worrying about the price."

"You only live once, right? Don't worry about where the money is coming from. I'm retired now and living comfortably off the investments I made during our heyday."

"*Your* heyday."

This was always a bone of contention between the two, and it had kept them at arm's length for all these years.

Aria had been a cop before she decided to take up vigilantism. She "borrowed" her logo from Midnight and used his alter ego's name to inspire her own: Luna.

Initially, Midnight didn't appreciate his symbol being lifted and used without permission. But when he saw the good Luna was doing in her neighborhood, he came to see the aping as a compliment. The physical size difference between the two meant no one would mistake one for the other. Plus, it wasn't like there was anyone he could lodge a complaint with anyway.

Her extracurricular activities interfered with her day job, and she was dismissed due to her frequent absences.

Midnight tried to help where he could by giving her equipment and supplies she couldn't buy anywhere even if she'd had the money, but that didn't put food on the table. Luna began freelancing as a bodyguard to the rich and famous who loved being seen and photographed with a real-life costumed vigilante by their side. Midnight was uneasy with this blurring of lines. An incident concerning the missing jewelry of one of her clients, followed by Luna's recovery of the jewelry, made Midnight feel as though Luna was becoming more of an enforcer than a bodyguard.

He confronted Luna about the situation. Needless to say, she didn't feel the same way as he did, nor did she appreciate him questioning her movements. As far as she was concerned, what Midnight did was no different, and he had no right taking the moral high ground.

"So, did you ask me to dinner just to get an old tracking device back, or was it really to go through my finances?" Aria asked.

"Sorry, old habits, I guess. It's none of my business now anyway."

"It wasn't any of your business back then either."

"I was just trying to look out for you. You know I—"

"Wherever did you get the idea that I needed looking out for?"

The directness of this question caught Simon off guard, causing him to almost choke on a sip of water.

"I'm sorry." Aria exhaled.

"It's fine. I probably deserved that. I want you to know, though, that my concern has nothing to do with my opinion of your skills. I still think you're one of the best"—Midnight saw the waitress approaching with their drinks and quickly found a word other than vigilante—"people at what we *did*."

The waitress set their whiskeys down and took their dinner orders. The two waited until she was out of earshot before continuing their conversation.

"Do you know what I was thinking about the other night?" Aria asked. "Do you remember that time we took down The Tank?"

Simon nearly spit his sip of whiskey back into the glass while trying to stifle a laugh. "I haven't thought about that in a long time."

"I think about it all the time. I messaged you saying I'd tracked down the indestructible metahuman that'd been robbing electronics stores in the neighborhood. I climbed in through the fire escape and found piles and piles of DVD players, back when a DVD player cost a month's rent. It was him, I was sure of it, *but...*"

"But you wanted backup."

"That's right. I knew I could handle him no problem *if* I could catch him without his metabands powered up, but if I couldn't, I knew you were the kind of guy with the right gadget to take him down."

She had been right about that, although the timing had been lucky. Midnight had gone up against a metahuman, Big Boy, with the same abilities just a week before. That metahuman had been a bodyguard for a mobster named Little Sal, who Midnight had needed to get to for information about a missing person.

Day and night, Big Boy was never more than five feet away from Little Sal. Little Sal knew Midnight was coming for him, and he'd hired on additional bodyguards. They were stationed all around his property. Midnight knew he could work his way through them, but not without alerting Big Boy and him powering up his metabands.

He'd taken a chance in assuming the metahuman was still vulnerable to gas attacks, guessing that Big Boy's powers were limited to his muscles and bones, not his lungs and brain.

Midnight had been right and lucky. Little Sal had twice the number of guards as Midnight's highest estimate, and they spotted him within minutes of entering the grounds, forcing him to fight his way to Little Sal. The gas actually worked a little too well, knocking out Little Sal before Midnight could get the information he needed. He had to revive him with smelling salts while approaching police sirens wailed in the background.

"You thought the same thing would work with The Tank, remember? You were so confident that your silly knockout gas was the perfect way to get in and out without any trouble," Aria said through her laughter. "But the gas never made it into the room where The Tank was."

Simon smiled and nodded. He remembered it all, but he let Aria finish recounting the story. He liked the way she told it, and he liked to hear her laugh.

"As long as I live, I will never forget the expression on The Tank's face when you kicked open that bathroom door. He had absolutely no idea what was going on."

They'd literally caught The Tank with his pants around his ankles. As soon as he saw the masked Midnight in his busted doorway, he leaped for the sink, where he'd placed his metabands before he started doing his ... business.

However, he must have forgotten that his pants were around his ankles, because he only made it one step before he tripped and his feet flew out from under him. His head struck the corner of the marble sink so hard that Midnight and Luna thought he was dead.

"Do you remember what you said after you were sure he was alive?" Aria asked.

"I hadn't counted on a counter-gas attack."

Aria laughed so hard that it drew stares from nearby tables. For the first time in a long while, Simon was having such a good time that he didn't care about attracting attention.

NINE

Amanda was bored with eating ghosts. Before tonight, she couldn't have imagined finding herself bored when she had an entire arcade to herself, but here she was. The problem wasn't that she was bored, but that she knew Lily was out there somewhere and probably needed her help. It was impossible to stop thinking about, let alone enjoy herself, despite the electronic distractions.

Simon's instructions had been clear: the safest place for her was the arcade. But that didn't make sense. People who had it out for Simon had already visited the arcade. And as far as Amanda knew, no one was looking for her. She was just the friend of a missing girl and asking a lot of questions at a pawnshop. Simon was likely the one they were really after, and he thought it was just fine for him to leave. Once Amanda talked herself into something, she rarely backed down.

Lily was out there, and she needed to sit down and talk with her. That was something they were always so good at: talking things through. There was a trust between them, even before their metabands came into the picture. No matter what Lily was going through, Amanda was positive it was something they could figure out together.

It was Saturday, which meant there was a Receptive introductory meeting tonight. She remembered Lily going to one before she disappeared.

Amanda glanced up at the clock above the token machine. Simon hadn't told her where he was going, but based on his clothes and the instructions he'd given her about not leaving, she assumed he'd be gone for a few hours, if not longer. She could go to the meeting and be back before Simon returned. The meetings were only an hour long, and if it became obvious it wouldn't provide any leads, she could split.

The more she let her brain work on the problem, the more she convinced herself that even the smallest clue or lead about Lily's whereabouts was worth the risk.

Her mind was made up.

She left Ms. Pac-Man in the middle of the maze as the ghosts moved in to surround her, and headed out the door.

"WELCOME, WELCOME, COME RIGHT IN," the man holding the door said as Amanda approached.

Amanda flashed a polite smile and entered.

"Is this your first time here?" the man asked.

Amanda nodded.

"I didn't think you looked familiar. Well, all are welcome here," he said with a smile.

The man was middle-aged with a slight beer gut. He wore khakis and a button-down shirt and struck Amanda as very plain looking. She was sure she couldn't pick him out of a lineup of older white guys if you paid her, but he seemed nice enough. As soon as the thought hit her, she put her guard back up. In her experience, people who went out of their way to seem nice to strangers rarely were.

"I'll walk you down and introduce you to everyone," the man said. "I'm Jeremy, by the way. I'm one of the discussion leaders here at the center. Right this way ..."

Jeremy led Amanda down a fluorescent-lit hallway.

"I apologize for the location," he said.

"I thought this was always where meetings took place?" Amanda replied.

Jeremy gave her a quizzical look. "So, you have been here before?"

"What? Oh, no. A friend of mine used to come here sometimes."

"Ah. Well, we're moving to a new location soon. Much better facilities. It's all very exciting. Who is your friend? Perhaps I know her?"

Amanda mentally reprimanded herself. She'd been here for thirty seconds and had already referenced Lily. So much for discretion.

"Saundra," her mouth blurted without checking with her brain first.

"Hmm, I don't recall a Saundra."

She wasn't sure how long Jeremy had worked here and whether not recognizing a name was common or setting off alarms inside his head.

"Anyway, it doesn't matter. We welcome everyone who has an open mind and an open heart," Jeremy said.

He led her to a room with the door already wedged open with a doorstop. He motioned for her to go in while he wrestled the doorstop from the door and shut it behind him.

The setup was what Amanda had expected: a circle of

chairs, with an urn of coffee and Styrofoam cups placed on a table in the corner. What she hadn't expected was the number of people there. The room was packed, the circle spread as wide as the room would allow, with people practically sitting on top of each other.

The people in attendance ran the gamut as far as age, race, and gender were concerned. They looked like they'd been sourced from generic stock photos that companies used in their marketing when they wanted to seem diverse.

They were all staring at Amanda, which made her even more nervous. She told herself they were simply observing the new person in the room. Although they were smiling, the smiles looked forced. Maybe it was just paranoia. After all, wasn't this how most religious types acted and behaved when they were looking to recruit a new member? They wouldn't add many members to their ranks if they greeted people with a scowl.

There were two empty chairs situated across from each other in the circle. Amanda assumed one of them belonged to Jeremy, but she wasn't sure which.

"Feel free to take either of the empty chairs," Jeremy said as if he'd read her mind.

Amanda chose the one farthest from the door and immediately regretted it. If this place was as weird as it felt, then she wanted to be closer to an exit, but it was too late to get up and change seats without it looking odd.

"Is there anyone who would like to start us off tonight?" Jeremy asked the room.

A middle-aged woman lifted her hand meekly. Jeremy's face lit up, and he gestured for her to speak.

"Hi, I'm Marie," she began. Jeremy motioned for her to raise her voice so the rest of the room could hear her. "I'm Marie, and I'm not really sure if this qualifies—"

"There's no such thing as a topic or expression that doesn't qualify, Marie," Jeremy said. "Metahumans have affected us all in different ways, both by their arrival and their absence. There's no right or wrong way to feel about them, just as there's no right or wrong way to feel about each other. All our experiences and feelings are valid here."

Marie nodded and continued. "I'm not sure why, but I miss seeing them up there in the sky."

There was a round of solemn nods from those who agreed or identified with Marie.

"I mean, when it all started out, it was the strangest thing in the world to look up and see a man or a woman up there, flying around. It felt like a strange dream or something you'd see in a movie. If you'd asked me back then if that was something I'd ever get used to seeing, I would have laughed at you.

"And I never did get *used to* seeing them up there, mind you. But over time, it became less strange. Then, on the day, when all those metabands stopped working, I saw it."

"Saw what, Marie?"

"I saw one of them fall from the sky. One of the metahumans. I didn't see where he landed, but he was so high up. I knew right away the fall would kill him, but I still watched him all the way down. I couldn't help myself. I couldn't look away, even though I wanted to.

"I still look up at the sky and expect to see one of them zip by. But they don't anymore, and I don't think they ever will again. And I'm not sure why, but that makes me afraid. It doesn't even make sense. I lived on this earth for forty-seven years before they appeared out of nowhere. Forty-seven years of looking up at the sky and expecting to see only birds and airplanes, and somehow, that isn't enough anymore."

"You don't have to make excuses for your feelings, Marie. We've all been through a trauma. The entire human race has. There isn't a blueprint for how you should feel about this because you're literally part of the first group of humans to ever experience it.

"That's what these meetings are all about: finding answers together and knowing we aren't alone in these strange feelings we're *all* experiencing, and don't let anyone tell you they're not. Thank you for sharing your feelings with us today, Marie. I know we all appreciate it."

That was the group's cue to applaud, and they didn't miss it. Everyone, that was, except for Amanda. The applause snapped her out of what felt like hypnosis.

She hadn't heard anyone express their feelings about metahumans in such an honest and open way before. The television and newspapers had all taken positions as either relieved or devastated by the departure of metahumans. "Menace or saviors?" was the question of the day, and how you answered it determined how you felt about their absence. This woman, Marie, presumably didn't have a personal connection to metahumans. She was just an ordinary person trying to go about her life the best way she knew how, both before and after super-powered flying people started popping up around the world. Her experience and feelings were more common than most would assume.

"Is there anyone else who would like to share tonight?" Jeremy asked. His eyes lingered on Amanda longer than on anyone else. She quickly averted her eyes in case he was about to call on her to speak.

"I'd like to talk, if no one else wants to," a bespectacled man a few seats down from Marie said softly.

"Of course, Lawrence. Please share."

The man stared at the floor for a few seconds, and Amanda thought he'd lost his nerve. She expected him to wave off the attention and insist Jeremy pick someone else, but then he began to speak.

"A lot of you probably recognize me. I come here a lot, just to listen," he said, his eyes still pointed toward the linoleum floor. "But I appreciate hearing everyone's opinions and feelings. I really do. I'm not always sure why it helps, but it does."

There were a handful of appreciative smiles around the circle. Lawrence peeked up and noticed them. He readjusted himself in his seat, gaining a small degree of confidence now that the hardest part, speaking up in the first place, was over.

"I was a metahuman," Lawrence said.

Reflexively, Amanda scanned the room. She wasn't sure how the rest of the room would take that revelation. She wasn't certain if the group would turn on him or if this previously unacknowledged information would be welcomed or not. The meeting wasn't billed as a place for former metahumans to offer support to one another, although groups like that existed.

But the room didn't change. If those seated next to Lawrence had a reaction to this revelation, they didn't show it. Instead, they patiently waited for Lawrence to continue speaking. Amanda wondered if others in the room had already known or figured out that Lawrence had been a metahuman. Before she could spend too much time contemplating that idea, her brain moved on to a new one: Who else in this room might be a former metahuman?

"Actually, I don't know if that's necessarily accurate," Lawrence said.

"There are no right or wrong answers here, Lawrence,"

Jeremy said. "Maybe you can share with us why you aren't sure if you were a metahuman?"

Lawrence took a deep breath and stared up at the ceiling tiles as though he'd written what he wanted to say on them before the meeting began. The pause lasted so long that Amanda couldn't help but glance up just to make sure.

"When metahumans first appeared, I became fascinated with them. I read everything I could get my hands on. I watched all the TV specials. The news was on in my house twenty-four hours a day because I couldn't stand the thought of missing something. I almost lost my job because I was so distracted at work, looking out the window hoping to catch a glimpse of one.

"After a while, my fascination turned into something of an obsession. I didn't want to just know everything there was to know about them. I wanted to be one myself."

"That's a perfectly normal thought," Jeremy interrupted. He looked around the room so the statement wasn't just directed at Lawrence. "Who hasn't thought of becoming a superhero, even before we knew metabands existed?"

There was polite laughter. Lawrence cracked a smile, but Amanda could tell he was still thinking about what he wanted to say, carefully choosing his words.

"I started going out on these walks at night, after work. In the beginning, I told myself it was mainly for exercise, but I knew I was going out there because someone said they'd seen metabands fall from the sky and land somewhere in the woods behind the housing development I lived in.

"For months, I spent every night out there. I was worried they would get covered up by leaves or some woodland animal would find them and hide them in some hole. So I just kept going out, every night, convinced if I didn't find them, someone else would. That was something I wouldn't be able to live with.

"At first, my search was haphazard, but I soon became neurotic about making sure I'd checked every square inch of the woods. I found topological maps of the area, but they were out of date by decades. I began updating the maps myself, bringing them out with me at night along with a pencil and a headlamp. I would meticulously mark the spots I'd already checked, only to double back and check them again to make sure I hadn't missed anything.

"Then one night, when I dragged myself back home exhausted, I couldn't sleep. I sat awake in bed, going over the areas I'd checked that night over and over again, tossing and turning. By the time the sun came up, I'd already talked myself into calling in sick from work. I told myself I wouldn't be very productive on an hour or two of sleep anyway, so I might as well use the day more wisely by looking for metabands out in the forest.

"And then the craziest thing happened: I found them. They were resting against a tree trunk I must have walked by a thousand times. Somehow, I'd missed them every time, but that day I walked toward them at just the right angle, with the sun shining on them in just the right way."

"How did it make you feel, seeing those metabands lying there after searching for them for months?" Jeremy asked, noticing that Lawrence was staring off into the middle distance, obviously lost in his memories.

"I couldn't believe it. I just couldn't believe it. It seemed like the rest of the world had stopped spinning and it was just me and those metabands. I actually got scared because I thought my mind was playing tricks on me. It'd happened before. I guess sometimes when your brain wants something so badly, it'll pretend it's there just to see if you'll stop looking. And at that point, I wanted to stop. My life was unraveling. I wasn't eating or sleeping. I knew my boss was going to fire me any day now, but I just couldn't do it. I couldn't bring myself to stop looking. I'd almost given up hope of finding those metabands and almost stopped believing they existed. But I couldn't give up looking because I didn't know what I would do with myself every night if I stopped.

"So, after staring at this pair of metabands for what felt like an eternity, I finally ran over and picked them up. I couldn't believe how light they were. I'd read about that, so I thought I already knew what they'd feel like, but it was hard to understand it until they were sitting in my hands."

Lawrence got quiet again, and his thousand-yard stare returned. Jeremy let the moment rest, but after an awkwardly long silence, he pressed on.

"What happened with the metabands, Lawrence?" he asked, already knowing the answer.

"They worked," he said, staring down at the floor again. "I knew they weren't fakes because they looked so unusual. Their color, the way they shone in the sunlight. I put them on and hit them together and I could feel it. I could feel them working. I could see them tightening around my wrists like they were fusing with my body. It was the most amazing feeling I'd ever experienced in my entire life. All that time in the woods, my obsession, it was all worth it now that I had my own pair of metabands that no one could ever take away from me.

"But then something went wrong. The metabands relaxed their grip on my arms and slid off, landing in the mud. I picked them up, wiped off the dirt, and then I ran home. I hid them underneath my shirt, afraid if someone else saw them, they'd try to take them from me.

"I didn't think they were broken or anything like that. I just thought I was doing something wrong. I'd been out in the woods all morning and didn't know what was happening."

"And what was happening, Lawrence?" Jeremy asked.

"The Battle. I ran home and turned on my computer, ready to search all the usual sources to see if I could figure out what I was doing wrong with my metabands. But the first thing that came up were photos and news of The Battle. By that point, it was already over, but the news was still catching up. The Governor had already flown Jones into the sun, but we didn't know that yet. News was just beginning to break on metabands no longer working all over the planet, but no one really knew what was happening.

"But all of a sudden, I knew. I could feel it in my gut. I knew this was real. I knew this wasn't just some temporary problem. In my heart, I knew my metabands would never work again."

Jeremy looked as though he was going to ask Lawrence another question, but he thought better of it. Instead, he gave him a moment to collect himself.

"They were gone. I'd only just found them and they were gone. I started crying, then I started screaming. I must've broken every single fragile thing in my home and a few things that weren't so fragile. I was angry. I'd worked so hard to find these things and to have them ripped away before I ever got a chance to experience them felt so unfair."

Lawrence began sobbing, and Jeremy took that as his cue to take back the spotlight.

"It's okay to cry," Jeremy told Lawrence before addressing the entire room. "That goes for everyone, obviously. It's okay to feel these feelings. It's okay to feel jealousy and sadness. We should never bottle these feelings up or save them for another day. We should allow ourselves to feel these feelings so we can turn them into something good. That's the only true way to get past them."

TEN

"So, do you ever go out?" Aria asked Simon as they exited the restaurant and walked down the street.

"I'm out right now," he replied.

"That's not what I meant and you know it. I mean *out* out. With the mask."

"No."

They walked a few steps in silence. Simon could feel the next question coming.

"Why not?"

"It's not necessary."

Aria laughed dismissively. "I know you're helping out the girl and all, but I wasn't aware that crime left the city as soon as the metahumans did."

"You misunderstand. I help where I can, but I don't need the mask to do that."

"That's not true and you know it. I never liked wearing the mask. It was itchy, uncomfortable—"

"I offered to make you a new one."

Aria smiled at the memory. "Yes, you did, and I appreciated that, but that isn't my point. The mask was uncomfortable, but I wore it because it protected my identity, which let me do things I couldn't do otherwise. You know there are things you can't or won't do because you aren't willing to wear the mask anymore. Hell, my mask didn't even have half the fancy-pants tech yours did and I still used it."

"It's different now. The mask felt right before, but it doesn't anymore. The metahumans are all gone. Wearing the mask feels like trying to hold on to a time that doesn't exist anymore."

The pair approached the park that ran between the east and west sides of the city.

"Can I ask you something?" Aria asked.

Simon nodded.

"This is embarrassing, and maybe it's the wine talking, but ..."

"How come nothing ever happened between us?" Simon asked, finishing her sentence.

"You really do seem to have ESP sometimes."

As they walked, Simon looked for the right words.

"There was too much else," he finally answered.

"Well, that's pretty vague."

"It's purposely vague because I mean it in every sense. There was too much else, and not just for me, but for both of us. Too much that needed to be done. Too many people counting on us. Too much to lose if either of us lost our focus. I'm not saying it was a good or bad thing, but it was the hand we were dealt."

Aria stepped in front of Simon so they stopped face to face, only inches apart.

"And what about now?"

"What about now?"

"Is there *too much else* now?"

She glanced at Simon's lips before meeting his gaze and leaning in to kiss him.

"Is this a normal job, or have they gotten to you as well?" he asked.

Aria stepped back, looking almost wounded and embarrassed that he hadn't been thinking or feeling the same way.

"What are you talking about?" Aria asked.

"Alastair Green. Did he hire you, or are you a true believer?" Simon asked.

Aria's chock shifted into a smile. She sighed and shook her head. "It was because I asked you about the girl, wasn't it? You didn't mention her."

"That's when I knew for sure, but I had my suspicions all along."

"Then why did you play along?"

"I wanted to see you. It's been a while."

Aria stepped away, turning her back on Simon. She was running through her options and composing herself. She turned back, arms crossed.

"This is stupid, Simon. Just tell me where the girl is."

"You know I won't do that."

"I do? Are you sure? Because whenever I think I know you, you surprise me."

"Says the person who met me under false pretenses."

"They weren't false pretenses," Aria shot back defensively. "I was worried about you. I've been worried about you since all this happened. I wasn't sure you'd survive in a world without metahumans."

"I'm doing fine, thank you."

"Simon, this is ridiculous. You obviously don't want to be a hero anymore—that's why you put the mask away. You can have a normal life. It's entirely in your hands. You know that girl is a criminal, don't you?"

Simon nodded. "Was."

Aria sighed again, this time in frustration. "Damn it, Midnight. Just tell me where the girl is and this can all be over. She's a criminal, and she deserves the punishment that's coming to her."

"That's not for you to decide."

"I'm sure they would deal you in on the bounty. Hell, I'll give you a piece of my cut."

"You know that doesn't interest me."

"I do, but it was worth a try. Plus, it gave my associates more time to get her out of that bunker you built under the arcade."

Simon's eyes narrowed.

"You didn't think I'd figure that part out? Come on. After all these years, I still might not know much about you, but I know you've always liked your hideouts. That's how I know you you're not truly done with this life. Who hangs everything up but builds a blast-proof bunker on the wrong side of town?"

"Someone who thinks of everything."

"Well, you didn't think of everything this time."

"I let my guard down. It won't happen again."

There was a bright flash and a pop. On instinct, Simon dove. Two sparking electrodes narrowly missed his abdomen. He looked up from the pavement where he had landed and saw the electrodes resting on the ground ten feet behind him. They were attached to thin metal threads that extended to Aria's handbag.

"Boy, you weren't kidding when you said you wouldn't let your guard down again. I suppose we'll have to do this the old-fashioned way, then, won't we?" Aria said as she dropped her now useless handbag.

She grabbed the side of her dress and yanked, ripping a

seam up the side to allow for a full range of motion. She was getting ready for a fight.

"You don't have to do this," Simon said. "Let me go so I can return to Amanda before anyone gets hurt."

"Sorry. They sent me to delay you, and I'm not done delaying yet. Besides, they're paying me a bonus for every minute I keep you here."

Simon returned to his feet and put his hands up in a fighter's stance.

"Now we're talking," Aria said with a smirk.

He had sparred with her in the past, but they'd never fought in any kind of serious competition. That was about to change.

Simon thought about running. He had never run from a fight in his life, but this situation was different. He needed to return to Amanda as quickly as possible. He assumed it was too late to stop her abduction, otherwise Aria wouldn't have risked telling him about it, but the clock was ticking on her trail growing cold.

Before he could dismiss the thought of running, Aria blindsided him with a roundhouse kick. He stumbled back against the wall of the alleyway. Instinctively, his hands went up to guard his face, and he caught another kick inches away from caving his nose in.

Simon gave the foot a firm twist and sent Aria flipping through the air. Her foot broke free of Simon's grip, and she corrected her positioning in midair to land on her feet. She hadn't lost a step. If anything, she was quicker than he remembered. It was a reminder that he had lost a step or two during his premature retirement.

A flurry of punches came at him. He ducked and dodged all of them, except for the last—a haymaker that he stepped right into. He tumbled through the air, but he didn't catch himself as well as Aria had.

He landed on his left ankle, and it buckled under his weight and the odd angle he'd landed on, causing him to take a knee. Red-hot pain told him to stop putting weight on the foot, and he nearly screamed out loud.

He buried the pain under a grunt on instinct. It had taken him a long time to understand how important it was to never telegraph any weakness. Had Simon cried out, his ankle would still be in pain, but Aria would know it as well. Hiding the injury lowered the chances that she'd attack that area, although Aria was smart enough to know this and try to further weaken his ankle.

"Come on, Simon. I don't want to fight you, and you don't want to fight me. This could be a lot of fun under different circumstances, but there's too much on the line. Just stand down and we'll forget any of this ever happened. We can even go get some dessert if you want to. Personally, I'd kill for a tiramisu right now."

"Just let me leave, Aria. Your bosses don't need to know. You can tell them I got away," Simon said as he climbed to his feet, careful not to put too much weight on his injured ankle.

"My bosses? You're forgetting I'm freelance. I'm my own boss."

"Then prove it to me. Let me go."

"Sorry, I might be my own boss, but that doesn't mean I don't take pride in my work. I don't want word getting out that I can't complete the jobs I take."

"I had a feeling you'd say that."

Simon reached inside the front of his jacket and pulled out a small metal rod. He flicked it and the end telescoped out. Aria stopped moving forward, hesitant to take him on when he was armed.

"I always prefer a fair fight, but if you insist on using unfair advantages, then this is going to get messier than I would have liked," Aria said.

"No one ever said anything about fair," Simon answered.

With his eyes locked on Aria's, he drew his arm back and threw the baton. Aria flinched, but the baton wasn't headed for her.

It sailed over her head and hit the fire escape above with a loud clang. Aria looked up and saw Simon's true target: a rusted ladder attached to the fire escape overhead. The ladder, roughly ten feet long, fell at the speed of gravity. When it hit the end of its track, the rusted bolts cracked under the force and gave way. The ladder continued its fall, unencumbered by any attachments.

One of the legs, which was twisted and rusted into a sharp point, found its mark: the handbag Aria had dropped. The handbag was still attached to the two electrodes she had shot at Simon, and both electrodes were lying in a large puddle—the same large puddle Aria had just stepped into.

When the ladder hit the handbag, it punctured the large battery Simon knew was in there, delivering an electric shock through the electrodes.

The bag practically exploded, and the entire capacity of the battery discharged into the electrodes, the puddle, and Aria.

In less than a second, it was all over and Aria collapsed. Simon ignored the pain in his ankle and dove to catch her limp body before her head collided with the pavement. He moved his fingers to her carotid artery, feeling for a pulse.

It was weak, but he found it.

He breathed a sigh of relief. He hadn't known the discharge capacity of the battery. He'd taken an educated guess that it was strong enough to incapacitate, but not kill.

"I knew you wouldn't risk accidentally killing me, Aria," Simon said to her unconscious body. "Thanks for that."

Simon kicked the discharged battery into the corner of the alley. He then laid Aria down on the most comfortable looking trash he could find. She'd be out for an hour or so, and she'd wake up with one hell of a headache, but she'd be okay. He couldn't be sure about the same for Amanda.

ELEVEN

This is ridiculous. What a waste of time, Amanda thought.

She'd spent her entire night sitting in a basement and had nothing to show for it. The meeting was winding down, and people were gathering their personal items. A few were having conversations and moving toward the coffee urn, intent on hanging around longer.

Amanda decided it was time to admit this was a dead end and gathered her belongings to leave.

"Leaving so soon?" Jeremy asked as he approached her from within the mingling crowd.

"Um, yeah. I've got to get back before ..." She struggled to find a suitable excuse for rushing out of there, though she didn't owe this guy an explanation.

"That's a shame," Jeremy said. "We were hoping you'd spend more time with us."

"I would love to, but, you know, I've got to get going."

She pulled her coat on and started toward the exit, but Jeremy subtly moved to block her path.

"I know the first meeting can feel overwhelming. There's a lot of people and a lot to take in. That's why I think you'd benefit from hanging out a while longer. The conversations that happen after the meeting are more informal. You'll probably find that many people here share the same feelings you do and they're just too shy to express them in front of the entire group."

Amanda felt seriously uncomfortable. While Jeremy's attempt to keep her there wasn't necessarily threatening, she didn't like how he wouldn't accept "no" for an answer. Behind her, the stragglers continued their conversations. They laughed and greeted each other, which put her at ease. Jeremy could only go so far in keeping her here before he risked making a scene in front of dozens of people.

"Maybe next time," Amanda said.

"I think I know what's making you uncomfortable."

"I'm not uncomfortable. I just really need to go."

"You used to be a metahuman, and you're not sure how to feel about all this. You're not sure how to feel about the world changing around you overnight. You spent your entire life feeling like you never truly fit in, until you found that pair of metabands. That's when everything clicked into place."

"I'm not sure what you're talking about, but it sounds like something we can talk more about next time, okay?"

Jeremy deliberately sidestepped to block her path, this time less concerned with appearances. "Why don't you tell me why you're really here, Amanda?"

Shit. He knew her real name. Had she slipped up? Written it down by accident on the sign-in sheet they'd passed around?

"We're vigilant when it comes to our new members. When you make your organization open to all, it's important to know who you're letting into your flock and check that they are who they say they are. That's the only way we can make sure we haven't allowed a wolf into our sheep's pen."

Amanda was frozen in terror. Her first thought was to run, but the door she'd come in through was behind Jeremy. Would he chase her? How would he explain to everyone here why he was suddenly chasing a young woman out of the basement?

That's when Amanda's heart sank and her pulse quickened. She hadn't noticed it before, but everyone who had congregated around the coffee and cookies had gone completely, and totally, silent.

Amanda slowly turned around, physically trembling at the thought of what she'd find behind her. When she finally looked, she met the gazes of the two dozen attendees who had stayed behind after the meeting. Every single one of them had stopped talking and were staring at her, their expressions blank.

"There's someone who would like to meet you, Amanda," Jeremy said.

TWELVE

Simon ran into the arcade with abandon. His adrenaline was pumping, and he was prepared to fight his way through whatever he found inside. The interior was dark, without even the glow of the arcade game screens.

Simon pulled the fire alarm. Instead of triggering an alarm, the exterior metal shutter slammed down so hard it would have split someone in half if they'd been unlucky enough to be standing under it.

"No intruders detected," a computerized voice announced.

"Dammit!" Simon yelled.

He punched the side of the nearest arcade cabinet, splintering the wood, and ran up the narrow spiral stairs to the manager's office.

"Computer, playback the most recent intrusion."

"No recent intrusion detected."

"Play back the most recent exit," Simon commanded the computer.

On the monitor, he saw Amanda walking out of the arcade by herself.

"Dammit!" Simon yelled again. He'd given Amanda explicit instructions to keep her safe, and she'd chosen to ignore them. "Bring up current location: Amanda Khan."

"Tracker offline," the computerized voice came back.

Simon ran his hand through his hair, tugging when he reached the end. The small tracking device was nearly undetectable, even if you knew what to look for. It was also virtually indestructible, with multiple fail-safes. They didn't go offline on their own.

"Show last recorded location," Simon said.

The computer displayed a map of the city with a crosshair over Amanda Khan's last known location. Next to a series of coordinates, a background service displayed relevant information it pulled from an internet search on the coordinates. Amongst the stream of information, one piece of information stuck out.

The Receptive owned the building.

Simon stood at the desk, racking his brain for options. Amanda was gone, taken. If they were clever enough to find his tracking device on her hoodie, they wouldn't keep her in her last known location for long.

Simon was barely any closer to finding his device or Lily, and now the same people had possibly taken Amanda as well.

The time for half measures was over.

If Simon was going to find Amanda before it was too late, he would have to do it the most efficient way he knew how, regardless of the consequences.

SIMON SLID down the bunker ladder hidden inside the *Pac-Man* cabinet so fast he was basically falling.

He wasn't in the mood for precaution.

He moved down the low hallway to a locked room. The seam between the door and doorway was so tight, the tolerances so unforgiving, that most would have seen it as a dead end.

"Open," Simon commanded as he marched toward the door.

A complex network of face and voice recognition algorithms kicked in behind the scenes and verified his identity. The door unlocked, and Simon didn't even have to break his stride.

The door popped open as if it were pressurized from the inside. Simon had known when the time came to enter this room again, he wouldn't have time to wait. It was built on top of the hydraulic system that powered much of the hideout, including an untested feature that wouldn't stay untested much longer.

The interior of the vault was barely big enough for two people, but he'd never intended anyone else to enter it. Part of him had hoped he would never need it again, but he'd always known that someday he would. What's more, he had to admit that part of him, most of him, had *wanted* to enter this vault again.

He wanted to use these tools again.

He wanted to have a purpose again.

The black suit floated inside the vault as if held up by invisible fishing wire. But even Simon didn't have access to that type of technology. The suit was engineered to distribute its weight evenly and thus support itself—an important feature of this particular suit.

The earlier Midnight suits had looked similar. He didn't want the differences in his suits to be noticeable, lest they give his opponents any indication of a suit's unique function. Better to have his foes believe every suit was the same and that every suit could do whatever the latest rumor claimed.

This suit was different from all the ones before it.

The biggest difference was simply the time and care Simon had put into it. It'd been a major project of his for years, and since The Battle and the fall of the metahumans, he had thrown himself into perfecting it.

Many would assume that the suits he'd built to go up against metahumans were more defensive in design, but this wasn't always the case. The enemies Simon went up against were often stronger and near invincible. He could wear a suit made of tank armor, but up against someone like Jones, he might as well be wearing a t-shirt. Therefore, he built suits that accentuated his other advantages, such as speed or stealth.

This suit wasn't built to take on metahumans, and unlike other lightweight stealth suits he'd worn to patrol rooftops for street crime, there wasn't anything stealthy about it either. He'd built it with one thing in mind: keeping its wearer alive.

The inner layer was synthetic silk that replicated the tensile strength of a spider's web. It was stronger than steel and puncture-proof, as long as it wasn't shot at with diamond-tipped bullets.

The outer layer was a series of interlocking Kevlar plates that ensured the inner layer wasn't necessary. It also provided a buffer that helped soften impacts. Being bullet-proof meant little if your bones and internal organs were turned into jelly from concussive blows.

When Simon first found the property, he hadn't been aware of its most interesting feature. In fact, no one had been. It didn't appear on any of the city's blueprints because it was older than the city itself. Simon wouldn't have found it either if he hadn't been using radar to figure out the best way to expand the area beneath the arcade.

At first, he thought it was a false reading. After digging ten feet below the subterranean floor, he found that it wasn't a false reading at all. It was a vertical tunnel that ran hundreds of feet deep.

It was a shaft that had been used for mining or maybe as a well, and it looked over a hundred years old, if not older. Though it was partially naturally occurring, sharp edges had been ground down, and there were handholds that couldn't possibly be natural.

Finding oneself hundreds of feet below a city was a unique occurrence. The sub-basement was secure enough to not warrant digging any deeper, but still, this hidden feature had gotten Simon's brain working overtime on another potential use for it.

Now, he stood looking at the simple metal pedestal built to the exact circumference of the mineshaft. He hadn't yet fully tested the system. He'd run simulations, but not a real-world test. The necessity hadn't been there over the past year, but it was here now.

"Prepare Mark 27," Simon told the computer.

The suit turned 180 degrees, and a series of mechanical arms peeled away its layers like an onion. It was a flashy way to put a suit on, but it was also necessary since it required a fit and finish that he could trust with his life. Plus, it wasn't like Simon had someone to zipper up the back for him.

He stepped into the suit, and the mechanical arms sealed him inside the layers of protection. It was black like all his other suits. The color allowed Simon to blend into as many environments as possible during his preferred late-night hours. It also concealed the complex workings of the suit. Anyone close enough to notice that the suit was different probably wouldn't be conscious long enough to give it much thought.

The only discernible feature from a distance was the slim, stylized outline of a crescent moon emblazoned across the chest.

With the suit locked into place, Midnight stepped onto the metal pedestal.

His feet slid into barely visible grooves in the floor, each cut to match his boots. This served as a final form of security authentication, ensuring the machine couldn't be engaged accidentally by him or anyone else.

An electric current activated in the pedestal, causing a strong electromagnet to engage with the soles of Midnight's boots, locking the suit to the metal base.

The whir of the electromagnet paused as the hydraulic piston engaged, and in the blink of an eye, Midnight disappeared.

The hydraulic system was pulling the pedestal, as well as Midnight, down the well at a rate three times the speed of free fall. Midnight's suit kept him glued to the pedestal as he plunged deeper and deeper into the darkness.

Within a few seconds, he was at the bottom of the well, the pedestal in its resting position. The hydraulic system continued working to build pressure. Now it was just a matter of waiting a few more seconds, hundreds of feet below sea level, for the hydraulic pressure to reach its peak.

A short tone sounded to warn Midnight all systems were go, even though there was no way to stop what he had put into motion.

He took a deep breath and tilted his head upward.

Silence.

Then a deafening rush of air.

The hydraulic system released its stored energy, and the metal pedestal and Midnight shot upward.

Even with the suit in place, the gravitational force on his body was enormous. It felt like all his internal organs were in his feet as he rocketed upward.

There was a brief flash of light as the arcade's chimney opened to the outside world and then silence.

The suit's neckpiece and cowl were locked in place to prevent spinal cord injury. Stars and the moon pierced the darkness in front of him. His body climbed rapidly into the air, but his acceleration was slowing, and he would soon reach the peak of his ascent.

The neckpiece and cowl unlocked, allowing Midnight to look down.

The city sprawled below him. He could see the downtown skyscrapers. He could see the water's edge and the bridges out of the city. And he could see the building where Neil's home address was listed.

A second later, he reached the peak of his ascent and the next system engaged. The carbon fiber plates along Midnight's shoulder blades exploded off him in a blast of compressed air. A series of thin, light poles sprang out and clicked into place via a static charge. They formed a rudimentary hang glider over his head. The glider caught the air current, and a line leading from the wing to his belt caught him, preventing him from falling back down to earth.

As quickly as the glider formed, it shifted to bring its wings inward, forming a sharp V shape, and handlebars sprang out in front of him. He pressed down on the bar, bringing the glider into a nose dive.

He had designed this system for surveillance. Originally, it had been meant to launch an aerial drone, not a human being. But when it proved more efficient than he'd imagined, he'd retrofitted it to launch a person, specifically himself. He would never allow another person to use such a risky system, not that the opportunity would ever come up.

The glider was designed for single use. It was lightweight and wide to allow as much flight time as possible. The launch system was silent from the street, and the user was launched so fast that even if a passerby were looking in the right direction, they would see little more than a blur. Not that there was much in the way of passersby in the neighborhood—another intentional feature.

With an eye toward improvisation, he had designed the wings to be brought in close, allowing for a controlled but rapid descent.

The cowl highlighted the destination in his heads-up display. A reticular zoomed in on Neil's bedroom window, and another small interface displayed the heat signature inside the apartment.

Neil was alone, and unluckily for him, he was standing right near the window.

Midnight was close enough that his cowl had completed a facial scan. Neil kept staring at the patch of night sky that looked darker than the rest. Suddenly, it split into two roughly equal pieces.

One piece wasn't moving at all, as though it were hanging in the sky on a hook. But the other piece was moving even faster, like it was falling. It was also getting bigger, coming right at him. By the time he spotted the flesh-colored jaw, it was too late.

The window exploded into a thousand shards of glass that ricocheted off the walls, ceiling, and floor.

Neil had bigger things to worry about than cleaning up all the glass. His momentum kept changing where the floor and ceiling were as he tumbled head over heels. Finally, he came to a rest at the end of a long hallway, against the far wall of his apartment.

Gravity was acting funny again. His feet were off the ground, even though his back was firmly against the wall. Not only that, but he was still rising. He lifted his head, his face cut up and speckled with blood from the explosion of glass, and saw the darkness that had flown in through his window.

"Y-y-y ... you" was all he could get out of his mouth when he saw Midnight.

He was scared, but not for obvious reasons. He wasn't scared because a piece of the night had dropped out of the sky and crashed through his window. He wasn't scared because his home had been invaded and his personal space violated. He wasn't even scared of the blood, which he began to understand was his.

What he feared was the face in front of him. He could only see part of it, the rest obscured by a mask. Even the eyes were covered, marked only by two white voids. It didn't scare him that he couldn't see most of his attacker's face. What scared him was the part he could see.

The mouth.

The gritted teeth.

The anger.

It was the face of a man ready to kill to get what he wanted.

"Where is he?" Midnight growled.

"W-w-who?" Neil stammered out.

Midnight cocked his head, nonverbally asking him if this was how he wanted to play this. He tightened his grip to drive home the message.

"Compound."

"Where is the compound?" Midnight asked. He already suspected they'd brought her to the place he'd seen the blueprints for in Neil's office, but he hadn't found any information on its location. The Receptive's property holdings were a confusing tangle of shell corporations and false names. Pushing Neil for information was the most direct way to find out which of The Receptive's many properties was the one where Amanda was being held.

"I don't know. I swear. It's above my pay grade. They ... they keep it all separate, so the IRS can't keep track," Neil said.

"Do I look like the IRS?" Midnight growled. He squeezed Neil's throat even tighter, causing his face to turn a deep shade of red.

"I ... I don't know where it is. B-b-but I know who does," Neil squeaked.

ALAN ROBERTS COULDN'T FIGURE out where the noise was coming from. He'd always been sensitive to small noises, especially at night. It was why he'd had both the refrigerator and the central heating system replaced in his multi-million-dollar apartment multiple times. He couldn't stand the little clicking sounds. Usually, once he was asleep, he was out like a light. But this noise had been irritating enough to wake him from his slumber, and he was mad.

He threw his comforter off and stormed out of his bedroom. Alan paused in the hallway, his head cocked, listening for the sound again. Sure enough, there it was. A faint tapping. Alan suspected the heating unit again and marched down the hallway to find his phone. He didn't know or care what time of night it was. If he was awake, then the man who'd assured him this system was completely quiet would get a wake-up call too.

Alan paused before reaching for the kitchen phone. There was the tapping again, louder now, but it didn't sound like the heating system. For one thing, it didn't sound like it was coming from the ceiling. For another, the tapping didn't sound metallic. It sounded hollow, like tapping on glass.

He tiptoed down the hallway, ears perked toward the source of the tapping. He moved through the kitchen, heading toward the living area. The tapping was more erratic now. Alan turned the corner of the kitchen and found the source of the tapping. He'd been right about it sounding like glass.

There was Neil, tapping on the huge window pane that looked out over the city from the eighty-seventh floor.

Neil, however, was on the other side of the glass, outside the apartment. His arms were outstretched, clinging to the window. His legs were spread wide, each foot precariously balanced on the narrow ledge outside the window, which was not intended for a person to stand on, and certainly not from the eighty-seventh floor.

"Good God, Neil! What the hell are you doing out there?" Alan shouted as he hurried across the wide, dark living room to the window.

Neil's already wide eyes widened impossibly further. His brain didn't have enough time to process what that meant before pain completely overwhelmed him.

Right behind the pain was the sickening crack. Alan still didn't understand what was happening as he lost his balance and found himself face to face with Neil, with only an inch of glass separating them. The window flexed when

Alan's face hit it. It wasn't enough to knock Neil off the ledge, but it took a few years off his life.

Alan collapsed to the floor. He pushed himself up against the window, which was monumentally difficult until, suddenly, it became easier. Too easy in fact, as he wasn't standing at all. He was lifted off the ground and slammed against the window. Neil's distressed wails on the other side of the glass mixed with his screams of pain. Through the tears streaming down his cheeks, the world came back into focus.

"That was your fibula. The pain you're feeling is nothing compared to your femur breaking, which I will break next if you don't tell me what I want to know."

The voice was angry, almost inhuman.

But it was nothing compared to the face.

Half of it was obscured by darkness, which Alan realized was a mask. The eyes were pure white with no pupils, giving the entire face an otherworldly quality that further confused Alan. The lower part of the face was uncovered, revealing a strong, scruffy jaw and clenched teeth. Before he knew what was happening, his bladder had made a unilateral decision to release itself.

"Where is the compound?" Midnight growled.

His tone made it clear that "I don't know" wasn't an acceptable response, but Alan started saying it anyway. He didn't get past the first syllable before he felt tremendous pressure, followed by a loud pop.

His brain couldn't process the pain and began to shut down. His eyes were half closed when a slap across his face brought him back around. Alan looked down at his dangling legs and noticed that one was visibly longer than the other, held together by skin and muscle instead of bone.

"When I make a threat, I mean it. My patience is gone.

The next wrong answer will result in you joining your friend Neil on the ledge. I wouldn't put odds on you standing out there on one foot for long, so I'll ask you one final time where Alastair Green is before I decide you're useless to me, and you do not want to be useless to me."

Alan Roberts was one of The Receptive's wealthiest contributors. He'd long wanted a pair of metabands of his own, and he had bought into Alastair's promises of earning them hook, line, and sinker. In The Receptive, money not only increased your odds of receiving a pair of metabands, it also increased your access. Alan Roberts was an important person in the organization thanks to the money he'd donated. If anyone knew the compound's location, it was the man whose money was going toward building it.

"Okay, okay, please, I'll tell you anything you want. Just please don't hurt me anymore," Alan pleaded through tears.

"I'm not making any promises until I've heard what you have to say," Midnight growled.

"It's upstate. About an hour from here. Middle of the woods. No one knows it's there," he said.

"Is that where he brought her?" Midnight asked.

"Brought who?" Alan asked in return.

Before Midnight could say a word, Alan's face twisted in horror. This wasn't the response Midnight wanted to hear.

Alan fumbled for another answer, anything to stop him from breaking any more bones.

"No, no, wait, wait! Please don't hurt me. I really don't know who you're talking about, but if it's someone important, then that's where they would bring her. It's secluded. It's practically a compound. No contact with the outside world and armed guards all around the perimeter. Alastair said it's built to withstand and wait out the coming judgment. It's the most secure facility we have."

Midnight read the man's face. Sensors in his gloves reported his heart rate in the cowl's heads-up display, but the numbers were useless considering his condition. The only way to tell for sure if he was lying was by looking into his eyes, which were filled with terror and pain.

Midnight believed him, but he had to be sure.

He dropped Alan, which Alan hadn't been expecting. He landed on his shattered right leg and let out a scream that could wake the dead before nearly passing out from the pain again. He could see Midnight swiftly moving through the darkness, but only as a shadowy figure.

Alan prayed the answers he'd given Midnight were enough to make him leave. He started dragging his broken body along the windowed wall of his apartment, crawling toward the end table where the nearest cordless house phone was.

Neil's muffled screams from outside on the ledge alerted Alan, and he lifted his head in time to see movement through the dark living room. He ducked his head, and an instant later, he was showered in glass. All the air felt as though it were being sucked out of the room.

Once the glass had stopped falling, he raised his head and noticed he could hear Neil's screams clearly. More movement and hands were back on his chest.

Again, Alan felt himself being lifted off the ground. He looked down and saw his legs, one intact and the other destroyed, dangling eighty-seven floors above the city. His bowels joined his bladder in releasing.

"I need to make sure you're telling the truth, Alan. I want to believe you, and for your sake, you want me to believe you too. I don't want to have to drop you just to show Neil I mean business before I interrogate him again."

"D-d-directions to the compound are in my notebook inside the safe in my cl-cl-closet. The combinatión is 17-3-32."

Alan found himself effortlessly pulled back inside and discarded onto the floor. Black boots walked across the floor and disappeared into the darkness. A few seconds later, he heard Midnight ripping his clothes from their hangers, followed by the beeps of him punching the combination into the safe.

Alan quietly wept in the stillness, terrified the safe would malfunction or the coordinates weren't specific enough.

He waited for Midnight's footsteps to approach again, but the sound didn't come. After a moment of silence, he heard the crunching of glass behind him and jumped as much as he could in his broken state. He looked up and saw Neil, pale as a ghost.

"I ... I ... think he's gone."

THIRTEEN

Midnight ran up the service staircase. Sometimes, in high-rise buildings like this, the quickest way down was up.

He kicked open the door that led to the building's roof. It took him a second to get his bearings on the rooftop and figure out which direction was the quickest way out. On his way across the roof, he passed a rooftop helipad and thought about how much easier it would have been to fly in on a helicopter.

Alas, procuring a helicopter without leaving a paper trail was currently outside his ability, so he had to opt for a more mundane means of transportation.

"In position," a computerized voice announced through the earpiece in Midnight's cowl. It didn't need to elaborate further than that; Midnight knew what it was talking about.

He removed the grappling gun from his belt and aimed it straight out into the night. Rather than pulling the trigger, though, he thumbed a small switch on the grip. A small detonation from the bottom of the grip launched a barbed spike straight down. The spike embedded itself several inches into the concrete rooftop ledge.

Satisfied that the anchor was secured, Midnight pointed the grappling gun at the street below. His gloved finger rotated the barrel of the gun several clicks, locking a different projectile into the chamber. He took no more time than usual lining up his shot despite how high up he was. After years of practice, he'd found his aim was always best when he trusted his eyes and his gut rather than second-guessing the gun's sight.

Midnight pulled the trigger, and the gas-powered grappling gun shot a bolt from the barrel. Behind it was a long line of thread-thin carbon fiber. The line was one of the most expensive items in his exceedingly expensive arsenal, even though most would mistake it for black fishing line even on close inspection.

The bolt whistled toward its target: a nondescript black cargo van parked directly below. Half a second before the bolt collided into the roof of the van, the sunroof retracted, allowing the bolt to enter.

Inside the van, a strong electromagnetic plate positioned directly below the sunroof activated. The plate's magnet caught the bolt before it hit the floor, redirecting it in midair into a small hole that was the perfect size for it. Even from eighty-eight floors above, Midnight heard the satisfying clang of the bolt finding its mark.

A quick check on the gun confirmed the lock had activated properly, and Midnight was off.

He typically preferred diving when this high up. It allowed for a more controlled fall and redirection if needed. But he also rarely jumped from this height when he intended to reach the ground. That meant a feet-first fall, with the grappling gun line directing him to his landing point.

The carbon fiber line sang as the carabiner scraped

across it. Midnight pulled his arms in close as he sailed through the night toward the entry point of the van.

He cleared the opening and landed with an impact that tested the limits of the van's suspension system, not to mention his knees.

Once inside, the line detached from its anchor point and a pulley inside the van rapidly reeled it in. Midnight was in a hurry. Normally, he would have been satisfied to just leave the line behind, there was always more, but in this case, the less evidence he left behind, the better.

The end of the line cleared the roof's opening, and the heavy bulletproof glass closed with a solid thud. With the seal engaged, the hum of the numerous electronics filled the interior of the van, and the extensive array of computer systems lit up.

Midnight punched in the coordinates that Alan had given him, and the van lurched to a start. The autonomous driving system wouldn't get him to the compound as fast as he could drive himself, but it freed up his hands. According to the GPS, he had roughly an hour's ride and that time would be best used preparing.

He didn't intend to waste time once he arrived.

The driver seat had deployed a dummy that was realistic enough from a distance to fool other drivers. A series of RADAR and LIDAR sensors along the outside of the van would pick up the presence of police and automatically adjust the vehicle's speed and aggressiveness.

He didn't expect many encounters this late at night, but he could swap out the dummy and take the driver's seat in a matter of seconds. Otherwise, the van would be flooring it the entire way to the compound at speeds exceeding ninety miles per hour.

Midnight tapped a screen embedded in the van's interior wall, and the display showed the exterior view from the van's front windshield. He was pulling onto the freeway, meaning the speed of travel would increase exponentially as he exited the city.

He pulled a previously invisible drawer from the wall separating the front of the van from the cargo area. Everything in the interior was undetectable and hidden when not in use, allowing the van to avoid raising suspicions even in the unlikely event that he was pulled over.

The drawer held a keyboard and trackpad. A small, low profile chair rose from the floor and swiveled into position. He didn't bother removing his gloves before getting to work. Multiple windows and terminals opened in front of him, his fingers a blur as he worked.

Within moments, he had breached an NSA-controlled satellite that the public had no idea existed. The agency had launched it eighteen months ago to track flying metahumans around the world and deduce their civilian identities. They'd intended to use the satellite as a way to coerce less-than-willing metahumans to bend to their whims. The NSA, however, never worked out the kinks before The Battle. After The Battle, the system became useless, and they all but abandoned it.

Unbeknownst to them, Midnight had discovered the biggest problem as it related to correcting telemetry calculations and speeding up image transmission. The system had been designed to capture still images, but Midnight had optimized it to transmit low frame rate video in real time.

25,000 miles above, the NSA satellite in geosynchronous orbit turned on a series of small thrusters and relocated to the coordinates Midnight had fed it. The transmission cut in and out before reestablishing its connection and feeding the image to his display.

Alan hadn't been lying, which was a relief since he didn't want to turn back around. He had almost run out of ways to hurt him.

On the screen was a veritable fortress. A solid concrete structure surrounded by what Midnight assumed was barbed-wire fencing laid out like a maze. It bore little resemblance to the limited blueprints he had found in Neil's office. The areas were indistinct from one another for the most part, which would make finding Amanda more difficult.

He told the computer to zoom in on the gatehouse outside the compound, searching for anti-vehicle systems such as road spikes.

A red warning light flashed above his head.

"Law enforcement vehicle detected," the computer announced in an emotionless monotone.

The picture-in-picture window at the bottom of the van's wall expanded to take over Midnight's field of vision.

"Son of a..."

A highway patrol car was approaching rapidly enough that Midnight could already make out the two people seated side by side inside. He brought up another video feed showing empty highway ahead of them.

These patrolmen had simply been in the right place at the right time, and they didn't need radar to know the van was traveling at more than twice the speed limit. It was just bad luck, but he still cursed at the dummy driver.

"Recommended course of action required," the computer said, unable to take independent action.

"Deploy road spikes," Midnight said calmly and returned his focus to filling a pouch full of flash-bang grenades.

"Road spikes deployed," the monotone computer voice announced.

Midnight glanced up at the display to ensure the road spikes worked without flipping the police car. He had no interest in hurting innocent bystanders, but he couldn't spare a single moment either.

The road spikes resembled larger, sharper versions of the jacks children played with, or would have played with fifty years ago. They were coated with matte black paint to help them blend in with the highway and avoid detection, but Midnight could still glimpse their outlines as they bounced down the road toward the approaching squad car.

An instant before the cop car ran over the tacks, it swerved, narrowly avoiding them.

They might be hard to see, but they weren't invisible.

Still, this was a first for Midnight.

"Pull over immediately," a voice boomed through the cool night air.

It was coming from the speaker system mounted on the roof of the squad car. Midnight cursed under his breath. He had never drawn police attention when using the otherwise discreet van, and he was becoming annoyed. His annoyance was mostly directed at the AI systems controlling the van, though. Obviously, he'd have to tweak it if he wanted to use the van for high-speed autonomous transportation in the future.

He considered deploying another batch of road tacks but decided to save them. He still had a ways to go, and there was no telling what trouble he might encounter along the way. Odds were the driver of the cop car had already called in for backup, although Midnight's onboard systems hadn't picked up the call over any of the available police frequencies.

Midnight considered his other options. Both vehicles were traveling too fast for him to deploy the other options he had safely. Though he needed to get to where he was going as fast as possible, he wasn't willing to risk flipping a police car.

Just then, the police car rammed the back of the van, jolting Midnight forward. He fell off his seat and tumbled onto the van's floor. Looking up at the monitor, he saw the police car filling the entire frame.

This wasn't normal. Midnight knew police procedure inside and out, and while the rule book didn't say anything specific about what to do if a blacked-out van deployed road spikes, he knew that ramming the vehicle was too aggressive a move after only a minute of giving chase.

"There's only one way this ends for you, freak. Pull the van over now!" the man shouted over the PA.

These weren't just cops. They were Green's men. That was why Midnight's police scanner hadn't picked up their chatter.

They weren't calling for backup because they weren't here on police business. They were here to stop Midnight.

He had hoped he'd given himself enough of a head start before Alan found a phone. So much for the element of surprise.

On the other hand, these weren't innocent cops trying to stop a speeder anymore. They were now no different from the henchmen dispatched to his arcade. That meant the kid gloves could come off.

The car hit the van again.

Midnight wasn't caught off guard as badly, but the hit had come from the side this time. The police cruiser was attempting to push the van off the road and into a ditch.

Not a terrible way to try to stop him, but the van was too heavy for it to work.

Then came a series of pops. They were shooting at the van. One shot hit the side of the van, though with the bulletproof armor plating, Midnight paid it little attention. They must have aimed the other shots at the tires, which were similarly armored.

"Computer, open roof access hatch."

The motor pulled back the bulletproof tinted glass that separated Midnight from the outside world. The wind whistled into the van at over one hundred miles per hour. He placed his gloved hands on either side of the opening and pulled himself up.

He crouched on the roof of the van, the wind whipping his face and threatening to knock him over. He swiveled his head, seeking the patrol car, and found it a moment too late as it slammed into the opposite side of the van.

They'd built up more speed, realizing they would need it if they hoped to push the much heavier van off the road. The van veered wildly across multiple lanes as the tires squealed and the anti-lock brakes struggled to keep the van from skidding sideways.

Midnight lost his footing and tumbled over the side of the van. Reaching out a hand at the last moment, he found one of the disguised cameras mounted on the van's roof. They were not designed to support his weight, but they held, and he was grateful.

A loud pop exploded inches from his head and bounced off the side of the van. Across the highway, the driver had his service revolver aimed squarely at Midnight's head, his first shot having missed.

Midnight kicked off the side of the van and swung his

free hand around to grab the nearest handhold. He heard another pop, and pain exploded across his back.

Although the carbon fiber Kevlar weave of his suit kept the bullet from piercing his body, it still hurt like hell. But he didn't have time to contemplate the many different shades of black and blue this new bruise would turn. He needed to get back on relatively solid ground.

The shot had loosened his grip, and he almost tumbled onto the highway. He felt less confident about the suit's ability to withstand a fall at 100 mph than he did about its ability to deflect bullets.

It was time to make his move before a stupid mistake cost him his life.

Midnight planted his feet on the side of the van and pushed off as hard as he could. He vaulted onto the roof of the van and took a second to regain his balance.

The cop car swung around to the back of the van and dropped behind. The driver was looking to accelerate into the van with the hopes of knocking Midnight off it.

As the car sped toward him, Midnight saw the driver and his passenger clearly through the windshield. The passenger stuck his torso out of his window and aimed his shotgun at Midnight.

These two weren't looking to slow Midnight down. They were hoping to take him out.

Midnight reached for the grappling gun on his belt. Before he detached it, he discharged a single shot into the roof of the van from the handle. He winced, thinking about how he'd have to repair the hole. Not so easy when he was dealing with bulletproof material, but now wasn't the time to think about that. He grabbed the grappling gun off his hip and flipped a switch on the handle. The line he'd fired detached from the gun but stayed connected to his belt.

Then he leaped off the back of the van.

The eyes of the driver and passenger widened as he cut through the night sky toward them. In a panic, the passenger aimed and fired his shotgun, but the shot went wide. Midnight had been counting on him not being able to track his trajectory fast enough.

While still airborne, Midnight aimed his grappling gun. He fired, but the hook missed the cop car and dug into the asphalt behind it. The cops looked back and laughed. They stopped laughing a second later when the roof crumpled in, marking Midnight's landing. And they especially weren't laughing when another steel grappling hook shot down through the roof, embedding itself in the car floor between them.

Midnight crouched and pushed off the car, jumping as high as he could an instant before the line ran out of slack.

The cop car jolted to a stop as the rope caught, and both driver and passenger airbags deployed as the line nearly cut the cop car in half.

In midair, with only a fraction of a second to spare before he landed on the highway, Midnight flipped a switch on his belt and was yanked backward as the line retracted to the anchor point in the van's roof.

He hadn't jumped high enough to land on the roof, and he hit the back of the van with force. He grunted and pulled himself toward the access hatch, hoping this would be the only interruption in his journey.

FOURTEEN

The rest of the ride upstate went smoothly. Alastair Green's reach was wider than Midnight had assumed, but he hadn't infiltrated the full police department. If he had, additional cars and probably a chopper would have been on him.

The van continued its journey down the dark, quiet highway. The previously silent interior was now noisy thanks to the hole Midnight's grappling gun had put in the roof. The police scanner picked up a call for assistance from the car he'd totaled. The officers were both alive and talking, though they didn't mention what had nearly cut their car in half.

Midnight suspected they would have a lot of explaining to do once help arrived, including why they'd discharged their firearms without radioing for backup. Midnight was five minutes out from the compound. He was as prepared as he'd ever be, but his throbbing back reminded him that he wasn't even at his destination yet and he'd already been shot.

Highways melted into two-lane roads before becoming single lanes. He hadn't seen another car in a while. The police scanner remained quiet as well. Eventually, the paved roads gave way to gravel, and the onboard AI had too much trouble navigating them.

Midnight typed a command into the van's computer, and the wall separating the cab from the cargo area swiveled around as though it were spring loaded. He removed the dummy and took the driver's seat. Another press of a button on the side of the seat and it swiveled back into its driving position.

Midnight kept his cowl on despite how it might look to passing cars, but anyone he passed from here on out likely worked for Alastair anyway, so it hardly mattered. He also flicked off the headlights. The computer AI didn't need them since it relied almost entirely on infrared light, but a van flying down a highway at 100 mph without its lights on was bound to arouse suspicion. With suspicion no longer a problem, Midnight could rely on the night vision inside his cowl instead.

The van crept along the gravel road. When Midnight spotted the compound's lights, he pulled off the main road and drove as deep into the woods as he could safely go without getting stuck. Once parked, he reopened the hatch and scrambled onto the roof. He tapped the side of his cowl and a small pair of lenses dropped down over his eyes, magnifying his vision.

The building's exterior was quiet, as he'd expected. The compound was way off the beaten path, so it would be odd for a random passerby to stumble on this place, but if they did, they wouldn't think much of it from its nondescript exterior.

No fences, no guard towers, no spotlights. It occurred to Midnight that the best way to hide a prison was to make it look like something else. Still, he'd expected to find guards in place now that they knew he was coming.

Midnight waited, as still as a statue and with his all-black tactical suit blending in with the dark forest around him. His patience paid off when he spotted a lone guard patrolling the perimeter. Across his chest was the strap of an assault rifle, and he held the weapon firmly in both hands. Hardly the type of equipment one would expect at a "religious retreat."

The man appeared to be in his early twenties, and as he paced back and forth in front of the compound, he repeatedly looked down at his gun, checking that the safety was on and adjusting his grip. He didn't seem used to the weight as he kept shifting the strap across his shoulder.

This wasn't a guard. This was bait meant to draw Midnight out of the shadows. Still, this bait had information that would benefit him. He doubted the kid knew where they were keeping Amanda, but he would have a rough idea of how many men were waiting for him and how well they were armed.

The trick was grabbing the guard without drawing attention.

Midnight tapped his cowl again to dismiss the telescopic lenses and took in his surroundings again. After failing to find another route into the compound, he opted to take the path he'd spotted on his way in: going up. The tree nearest the van was close enough to hop onto from the roof, which he did with ease. This was convenient since deploying his grappling gun might cost him the element of stealth if he missed. He worked his way up through the branches, careful to make sure each branch could support his weight before pulling himself up.

Some time had passed since Midnight had found

himself outside an urban environment, and while the fresh air felt pleasant inside his lungs, he couldn't move through the trees as fast as he wanted. The guard's random patrol made anticipating the direction he needed to head in difficult.

Soon, though, he found himself within twenty feet of the man.

It was now or never.

Midnight reached into a pouch on his belt and fished out a small ball bearing. He flung the bearing as far into the forest as he could. It bounced off a tree trunk and landed with a sharp crack in a patch of dried grass.

The guard stopped in his tracks and nearly gave himself whiplash as he searched for the source of the sound.

He stood silently for a long moment, his eyes straining in the darkness. Clouds covered the moon now, and without night-vision goggles or similar technologies, he couldn't see more than a few yards in front of him.

Unsure what to do next, the young guard took the walkie-talkie from his belt and pressed the button on the side.

"Uh, I think I heard something," he said, his voice barely above a whisper. He waited for the response.

"What was it?" a voice from the other end squawked back. The walkie's volume was turned up to the max, and the guard nearly jumped out of his boots at the sudden loud noise.

"I ... I ... I don't know. I can't see where it came from. It's too dark out," he stammered.

There was a long pause as the men on the other end of the walkie-talkie discussed what to do next. "Go find it," a different voice replied.

"Go find it? The sound, you mean?"

"No, the lost city of Atlantis. Yeah, the sound, you idiot!"

The guard clipped the walkie back onto his belt, his hand shaking the whole time. He gripped his rifle in both hands and flicked the safety off. What this guard lacked in skill or bravery, he made up for in his ability to follow orders unquestionably. Midnight was starting to understand why they'd chosen him for this job.

While the guard offered little in the way of danger, an errant shot would alert everyone within a mile of his presence at the compound and his position. They'd know he was here soon enough, but any effort to delay that would be worth it.

Midnight stayed crouched high in the tree, his eyes never wavering from the guard. He watched as the man nervously approached the area where the sound had come from.

This path led him directly below Midnight.

And when the time came, Midnight pounced.

He dropped from his perch with his feet angled at the gun. His landing was spot on, and both feet hit the assault rifle simultaneously. His weight knocked the rifle from the guard's hands, and it remained firmly under his boots.

The guard's face contorted into what would either be a scream for help or a yelp of surprise. He cupped the guard's mouth with his right hand while his left forearm pushed the guard into the tree he had jumped out of.

"If you scream, this will end very badly for you," Midnight growled, their faces only inches apart.

The guard was even younger than he had expected. Late teens. The boy's eyes were wide and filling with tears. Midnight looked down and realized why. The rifle had broken the guard's right index finger when Midnight had forced it from his hands.

"That's unfortunate, but it'll be the least of your prob-lems in exactly ten seconds if you don't tell me what I want to know. Now you either pull yourself together and I'll take my hand off your mouth, or keep screaming and find out how much more it hurts to have all ten fingers broken."

The man understood and became very quiet. A calm-ness washed over his face.

"Good, that's much better," Midnight said. He removed his right hand from the guard's mouth. "How many men are in there?"

The guard's eyes glazed over, and he slumped against the tree. Only Midnight's forearm kept him on his feet.

Midnight shook him, but he'd seen enough unconscious people to know when someone was out cold. Whether he'd passed out from fear or the broken finger, Midnight wasn't entirely sure, although he suspected it was a combination of both.

It was time for Plan B before Plan A had even begun.

Midnight picked up the guard's assault rifle, and after a few quick movements, the weapon fell to the ground in pieces. He then took the firing pin and threw it as far into the woods as he could. When the guard came to, Midnight didn't want him to have a loaded weapon.

Midnight then patted the guard down and searched through his pockets for anything useful. He found no cell phone, no keys, no wallet. He assumed these items were all confiscated upon entering the compound so that no one could leave without Alastair Green's say so.

The only item of note, besides the radio, was a single black and white swipe card, which he quickly pocketed.

He then picked up the guard's unconscious body and

dragged it deeper into the woods, placing it behind a fallen tree so that it wasn't visible from the compound.

Midnight guessed he had minutes before the others realized the guard was missing. If he was bait, then they would expect him to check in soon. The guard's radio was now in Midnight's possession, which he hoped would offer him a brief heads-up once they were on to him.

With the guard's body hidden from view, Midnight approached the building.

He flipped through multiple view modes inside his cowl's HUD to detect any nearby individuals. He was alone. Along the wall was a single metal door with a card reader next to it. A small red light blinked on every few seconds. He approached the door, his head on a swivel.

It all seemed too easy, but Midnight also wasn't aware of the group's potential yet.

He produced the keycard from his pocket and swiped it through the terminal. The blinking red light changed to solid green, and he heard a soft click. He opened the door and ducked inside a spartan, concrete room. The ceiling was high, roughly spanning all three stories of the complex. It was lit from above by a single row of fluorescent light bulbs. The distance between the lights and the ground produced a soft light that bathed the room in an almost dreamlike atmosphere.

Other than the lights, the only other remarkable features were pairs of doors on the other three walls. A strange design for a room roughly the size of a two-car garage. Midnight was still pondering the room's layout when all three pairs of doors flew open and a dozen men with assault rifles rushed in.

They were covered head to toe in black tactical gear, including balaclavas, tinted goggles, and helmets. Each had a physique far more in line with what Midnight expected from armed guards.

They were trying to outshout each other as they screamed commands at Midnight.

Hands where they could see them.

Down on the ground.

Remove the mask.

As efficiently as they'd lured Midnight into a trap, they weren't as well coordinated when it came to capturing him. They were too excited. Too scared. They'd likely been waiting behind those doors for a long time, anticipating this moment, and now their adrenaline levels had peaked. This was Midnight's one chance, so he took it.

As he slowly raised his hands in the air, his right hand grazed the back of his cowl-covered head. The action was nearly imperceptible.

This motion triggered two actions that were about to happen in quick succession, but before they could, the men moved in to take him into custody.

Midnight smirked. He'd debated how long to set the time delay on the mechanism. He'd opted for a longer delay, hoping his targets would approach him, increasing the mechanism's effectiveness.

The man closest to Midnight moved in first without caution. They'd been trying to catch him for so long that he could no longer keep his eagerness in check. As the guard reached to grab Midnight's hand, the lenses of Midnight's cowl changed from a faint, ghostly white to jet black. At the same time, a small device the size of a quarter sprang into the air from a crevice near the shoulders of his suit. It spun in the air like a top, the two blades on either side keeping it aloft.

Then, it exploded.

Not the kind of explosion meant to cause injury and devastation, though. Instead, it was an explosion of light and sound. The hovering object ensured everyone saw the device and were looking directly at it when it activated. If it went off a second too late, some would assume it was a bomb and instinctively cover their eyes. A second too early and some might not be looking at it.

But the entire room had been staring straight at it when it detonated, resulting in total temporary blindness and deafness.

Midnight's eyes and ears were shielded from the blast, allowing him to carry out the next step while everyone else was temporarily blind and deaf.

Chaos and confusion reigned for almost a full minute before some of the guards regained the use of their senses. But by then it was too late. Midnight was gone.

The highest-ranking guard plucked his radio from his belt and called in what had happened.

"We've lost him," he said into the radio.

"Negative, team leader," came the response. "All entryways remain locked and secure. Target has not left the containment area."

The men all looked at each other in confusion, then in panic.

Midnight was still in the room with them.

One of the men looked up at the ceiling.

"Holy sh—" he began to exclaim.

A man, wrapped almost head to toe in rope with his mouth bound with tape, dangled from a hook in the ceiling. He was alive but unconscious.

"What the hell? How did that happen to him?" a guard asked.

"Wait, isn't that O'Brien?" another asked.

"I'm not sure. I didn't catch his name," said a third.

And then all hell broke loose.

The last guard to speak struck the two guards closest to him, incapacitating them. It was Midnight, who had managed to borrow O'Brien's uniform before stringing him to the ceiling.

In the confusion, the men had let their guard down. Midnight had five of the guards out cold before the first could mount a defense against him.

Midnight, in a blur of motion and violence, easily blocked the guard's blows. The guards' rifles were useless in close quarters, the odds of an errant shot hitting a comrade too great.

There were only two guards left, and they moved in on Midnight from either side. They hadn't been as careless as the others, considering their line of attack before approaching.

After hesitating, the man on Midnight's right moved in and threw a right hook. Midnight ducked his punch and stepped forward, using the would-be assailant's momentum to throw him over his shoulders and into the guard behind him.

The pair slammed into the wall and were knocked out cold.

"Murphy, come in," the voice on the other end of the walkie-talkie demanded.

Midnight raised his boot over the walkie and brought it down in one swift stomp, scattering pieces of plastic and metal throughout the room. He didn't want it waking up his sleeping friends.

He unclipped a security badge from the chest of a passed-out guard in case the badge he already had didn't work in the rest of the facility, but he noticed there were no badge readers inside this room. Where the readers should have been next to the doors were freshly painted square patches. The doors themselves had no handles or knobs.

Midnight considered breaking through the wall to determine if the internal wiring of the removed badge readers was still accessible. They were likely plated over with steel, though, and he didn't have time for that.

He produced a small capsule from his belt. He twisted the two halves and placed it on the door, near where the lock would be on the other side of the door.

The chemicals inside the capsule began to react, turning into an acid that ate through the door's metal frame as though it were wet paper. Once the acid had sufficiently eaten through the locking mechanism, a swift kick to the door opened it up.

Midnight discarded the pilfered guard uniform and headed deeper into the facility.

FIFTEEN

Midnight moved into the next room with caution, scanning the area with every sensor he had access to, as well as with his own two eyes.

The Receptive hadn't expected Midnight to get this far, and the room's occupants had left in a hurry.

The room looked like it could have been plucked right out of a standard office park. All the lights were on, as were the computer terminals.

The only thing missing were the employees.

Midnight detached the grappling gun from his belt and aimed it at the security camera in the far corner. He discharged the gun, and the grappling hook shattered the glass lens, the arm holding the camera in place now bent at an extreme angle.

Whoever was watching already knew Midnight was in the room, but he didn't need to give them any more information than that.

The line retracted into the gun, with the hook taking a piece of the wall out with it.

The rest of the compound would be regrouping and strategizing. It meant Midnight had a moment to plan his next move too. He brought up a terminal window on the nearest computer and connected with his server back at the arcade. With direct access to their internal network, breaking in was trivial.

Two alerts popped up in Midnight's cowl.

The first was that the home server's AI had found a schematic of the facility on one of the hard drives he was scanning locally. The server was interpreting the map and collating it with the areas Midnight had already visited. Once the two data sets were squared against each other, his cowl would be better equipped to guide him through the facility.

The second was that there was another person in the room with him. His suit's microphones picked up a muffled sound that matched the cadence and frequency of human breathing. A more sensitive secondary audio scan picked up the heartbeat, confirming the presence.

Midnight calmly continued typing at the workstation, making sure the other person was not aware of his new knowledge.

"Locate," Midnight instructed his AI in a barely audible whisper.

He glanced up as his visual overlay placed a marker on the other side of the room. It pointed to a large refrigerator across from a row of cubicles.

"Probability," Midnight said, slightly louder and more confidently than before.

"Ninety-five percent," the AI replied.

In one quick and fluid motion, Midnight drew the grappling gun from his belt and took aim at the large, stainless steel refrigerator door.

He fired and the hook sprang across the room, sending a stack of papers flying in its wake. The hook sank deep into the refrigerator door and pierced through the other side. The element of surprise would only be in play for another second or two at best.

The grappling gun drew in the line as he took a couple of running steps toward the refrigerator. He pulled the line with all his might, jumping into the air like an acrobat.

The hinges weren't built to take that type of strain, and the door was ripped clean off. It passed under Midnight, missing him by inches. He landed on his feet in front of the refridgerator.

There, tucked inside the refrigerator, was a small, skinny man. The terror on his face made his age hard to nail down, but he appeared to be in his forties. His eyes were wide, and his mouth hung even wider, desperately drawing in air now that the refrigerator's seal was broken. And he was about to use that air to scream.

But Midnight was on him too fast. A fraction of a scream slipped out before a gloved hand clamped firmly around his neck. His momentum pushed the man back into the fridge, all the shelves already removed, though it wasn't entirely empty. A jar of mayonnaise and another of mustard rolled out onto the ground and smashed open on the carpet.

"If you'd like to know what air tastes like again, you'll be smart and won't scream, got it?" Midnight asked.

The man, his face turning a deep shade of purple, nodded rapidly, his lungs struggling for air. Midnight eased his grip but kept the man pushed inside the refrigerator. He gasped and sucked in air.

"Why are you here?" Midnight asked.

"I was working late. The alarms went off and the doors all locked. I didn't know what to do. No one was answering any of my calls. Then I heard screaming and bangs coming from down the hallway. I heard a hissing sound coming from the door and thought it might be a bomb, so I hid in the safest place I could find."

"Where are they holding Amanda Khan?"

"Who?"

Midnight's grip returned, tighter than before. The man's eyes bulged out of his skull. He frantically shook his head.

Midnight loosened his grip ever so slightly. He wanted the man to know he wasn't screwing around, but he wouldn't be of any use unconscious.

"Wait, please. I don't know who that is. I swear. They keep the subjects in the containment area. We aren't allowed to interact with them. I'm not even supposed to know they're there."

"What do you mean, subjects?"

Panic crossed the man's face. He'd said too much, but Midnight hadn't given him much of a choice. He was weighing the repercussions of saying anything more, when Midnight slammed him back into the refrigerator.

This time, the back of his head hit the fridge. He'd have a nasty bruise in the morning.

Midnight didn't ask his question again.

"I just work here, seriously, I promise you. I don't buy into all this cult stuff. I'm just here for the paycheck."

"What do you do?"

"I'm a scientist. I studied metahumans and metabands for years for a private organization. After The Battle, the funding went away. No one was looking for researchers anymore. Then one day, out of the blue, I get a call from The Receptive, offering me work. Good money. Great money, actually. I had to sign an NDA before they even told me where this place was, but I was used to certain levels of secrecy when it came to metahuman research projects. No one ever wants anyone else to know exactly what they do and don't know."

"And what do you know?"

The man looked as though he might clam up again.

Midnight let out an exasperated sigh as he pulled the man out of the refrigerator by his throat.

"No, no, no, no, no! Please. You have to believe me. I can't. They'll hurt me."

"I'll hurt you worse. One way or another, you're telling me what I want to know."

Even through the opaque white lenses, the look on Midnight's face told the man he wasn't bluffing.

"The metabands," the man whispered.

"What about the metabands?"

"They still work."

"You're lying," Midnight growled.

Though this man had information that could help him, he was growing tired of the drawn-out interrogation. If he was going to start lying, then he would be of no use to him.

"I'm telling the truth. They don't work like before, but they do work. They're not completely dead like everyone thinks. We don't completely understand it yet, but there's something there. You can't power them up and fly around, but there's residual energy flowing through them. Our job is to find a way to tap that energy. I mean, can you imagine the implications? A free source of energy. Completely renewable and perhaps endless in supply. It could change the entire world, more so than metahumans did."

"How?" Midnight asked, still not buying what he was hearing.

"We found something. Or rather, Alastair Green found

something. Look, I know he's a whack job—all of us working here know that—but there's no denying the device he found is unlike anything any of us have ever worked with before. It's decades ahead of everyone else."

"Where did this device come from?"

"He won't tell us, even if we're stupid enough to ask. One thing about this place is that you don't ask questions."

"If you had to guess," Midnight asked while reapplying pressure to the man's throat.

"I really don't know. It's man-made. We're pretty sure about that. The design is sloppy. Or maybe not sloppy, but utilitarian. It doesn't look anything like metabands, so we just assumed that whoever made it wasn't the same persons, aliens, gods, or whatever you want to believe that made the metabands."

"Where is it?"

"They don't tell me that either. I've only seen it in person a handful of times during tests. Other than that, it stays locked up tight somewhere. I'm not even sure Alastair keeps it on the premises."

Midnight released his grip, and the man finally set his feet on the ground again. He reached up to massage his sore neck, but his hands didn't make it before Midnight shoved him hard into a nearby desk. He grabbed the back of the man's collar and dragged a piece of paper in front of him. He then grabbed a pen from a cup and pushed it into the man's hand.

"Draw it for me," he demanded.

The man switched the pen from his right hand to his left and got to work. His hand trembled the entire time, but he drew swiftly. He may not have seen the device many times, but it had obviously left an indelible impression on his mind.

After a few finishing strokes, he stood up straight and handed the completed drawing to Midnight. He regarded the drawing with a mixture of surprise and anger.

That device had once belonged to him.

SIXTEEN

The terrified man gave Midnight all the information he had. It wasn't much, but he pointed him in the general direction of the device. Midnight left the scientist in the office. He couldn't cause him harm, and it was either that or stuff him back inside the refrigerator.

Past the office was a long hallway barely wide enough to permit two people to pass each other without having to walk sideways. There was a lone door at the other end, but strangely, both sides of the hallway were completely blank, exposed concrete and nothing else.

Little made Midnight nervous, but this gave him pause. In a facility so far designed to trap him, the lack of features struck him as a bad omen. The scientist had claimed this was the most direct route to the center of the facility where Amanda was likely being held.

As Midnight carefully walked down the hallway, he kept an eye on his HUD for any anomalies. It alerted him to movement at the doorway on the other end of the hallway. Someone on the other side was disengaging the lock. Then the door slowly opened, revealing Aria.

Or, more accurately, Luna.

She was clad head to toe in black, an almost mirror image of Midnight. The back of her cowl allowed her long black hair through, but otherwise, their costumes were identical.

"Just like old times, huh, Midnight?" Luna said.

"Step aside, Luna," Midnight growled. It was more of a warning than a request.

"I don't think so. We have a very strict policy here regarding trespassers, and I don't remember you being invited."

"I'm not in the mood for games. Tell me where Amanda is and get out of my way."

"You still seem confused, Midnight. This isn't your home, and you don't get to make the demands around here, so I'm going to make *you* an offer. Turn around and leave, and no harm will come to you."

"Enough."

"Fine, have it your way."

Luna broke into a full-out sprint and launched into a jump kick. Midnight blocked the attack and stumbled backward. With Midnight off balance, she threw a flurry of punches and kicks. He blocked or dodged most of them, but every third or fourth blow landed.

Her suit was not as heavily armored as Midnight's. She had no need for protection against ballistics or knives since he wouldn't use either against her. But what her suit lacked defensively, it made up for offensively, as he was finding out.

A left hook landed like a sack of bricks on the right side of his face. The knuckles in her gloves were reinforced with brass, making them extremely hard and heavy.

Midnight hit the ground on his knees, only to be greeted

by Luna's left foot. The toes of her boots were also reinforced.

He flew backward through the air and fell onto his back, knocking the wind out of him. His eyes struggled to focus in the dimly lit hallway, but they did in time to see an airborne Luna approaching fast.

With nowhere to roll out of the way in the narrow hall, Midnight caught Luna's foot before it landed on his face. She was caught off balance and landed on her back on top of him, right where a guard had kicked him in the ribcage. Even though she was much lighter than him, he grunted in pain. As he clamored to his feet, she threw another flurry of punches and kicks at him. She was fighting harder than he had ever seen, and she wasn't pulling any punches.

Normally, Midnight liked his chances in this type of fight. An emotional fighter made mistakes. But Luna was a fighter who made few mistakes. Maybe she'd been holding back all these years against criminals. Maybe she'd never fought for anything like what she was fighting for tonight. Either way, he was in trouble.

A roundhouse kick caught him right in the jaw, and he spun in the air before crashing to the ground. He struggled to get back onto his hands and knees, but she was relentless.

A swift kick landed against his ribcage, knocking a scream loose from his body. Of course Luna had recognized it as a weak point and was exploiting it for all she could. Even through the armor plating, he was certain she'd fractured a rib or two. The accumulated injuries were slowing him down significantly.

His hands went out from under him, and he found himself sprawled on the floor again.

Behind him, he heard Luna take a step back, and he worried she was getting a running start to deliver another kick to his ribs. His entire torso tensed in anticipation, but the blow didn't come.

He slowly turned on his hands and knees to face Luna and spit out a mouthful of blood. She stood a few feet away, looking at him with pity.

She nearly had him beat. Another kick like the last and he'd be in danger of blacking out from the pain. The effort had exhausted her, though, and she was using the break in violence to catch her breath.

"Stay down, Simon," she panted.

"And here I thought you knew me," he puffed back.

"I do know you. That's why I don't want to kill you."

"What happened to you, Aria?"

"Nothing happened to me. It happened to the world."

Midnight considered summoning his last reserve of strength to tackle her. He couldn't fight her in his condition, but he might be able to restrain her. He nonchalantly moved his right hand toward his belt to retrieve a folding set of restraints, but her eyes tracked his every move.

"Don't do that, Midnight. It won't end well for you if you try."

"I just don't understand, Luna."

"Of course you don't. You never did. You were always so focused on your one-man mission that you never took the time to understand anything. Who were you doing all this for anyway? What has it ever gotten you?

"Do you want to know what it's gotten me? You already know about the cracked ribs, the broken bones, the black eyes. The external damage. The things that eventually heal. Sure, the injuries never heal completely. The breaks especially. I'm still reminded of when some thug broke my knee every time it rains and it feels stiff, but the injuries are easy to deal with.

"But what about everything else? I tried to have a normal life outside all of this. I thought I was doing the right thing. I thought I was helping people. All I wound up doing was hurting the people closest to me."

"It's hard. You knew it would be hard."

"That's easy for you to say. No one knows you. You're no one. You're just Midnight. 'Simon' barely exists. It's just a cheap disguise you use when you need something you can't get while wearing a mask. You never attempted to have a normal life. You don't know the costs associated with it. You never had to watch some maniac dressed like a circus ringmaster throw your sister from a building. You never had to hear the dying screams of someone you love. The coast guard never called you to inform you they found your boyfriend drowned at sea. You didn't have to pretend you didn't know why a man who can turn into a sea monster would target you and your loved ones.

"You might not see it yet, but Alastair Green is right. He's right about all of us. Metahumans and vigilantes—we're all the same. We're just in it for ourselves. We all want to feel as though we're different from the rest of humanity, that we somehow know better."

"I've never thought that way."

"Yes, you do. If you didn't, you wouldn't have put the mask on again."

Realizing the hypocrisy in what she was saying, Aria lifted her hand to her face and removed her mask, dropping it behind her.

"I'm tired, Midnight. Aren't you tired?"

Midnight said nothing.

"You can stop this madness. You can be a part of this. A part of us. You know in your heart that Alastair is right. I didn't wake up one day and realize everything I thought I knew was a lie. It was gradual. Alastair understands that. He knows his teachings take time to process, especially for people like us. That's what makes him so special. He's patient with us, with the entire human race. He knows the human race doesn't have a future without us."

Midnight slowly pulled himself up. His leg shook as he dragged it under him. A combination of pain and exhaustion took turns battling his willpower, but he finally rose onto a wobbly knee.

"Maybe you're right, Aria."

It was Aria's turn to stay silent. She gave Midnight the time he needed to think before he spoke next.

"I've been fighting my entire life, and what do I have to show for it? I never asked for anything in return. Nothing. I'm tired. I've been fighting too long. Maybe it's time I listen to someone else's ideas. I can't promise I'll change, but I can at least listen."

Aria looked down at Midnight with tears welling in her eyes. She stepped toward him and knelt so she was at eye level with him. Once there, she looked deep into his eyes through the milky opaque lenses fitted into his cowl.

Aria stood and stepped back. She then reached for the gun hidden behind her back.

"I'm sorry, Midnight," Aria whispered as a single tear rolled down her cheek.

She pointed the gun at Midnight

"I am too, Luna," Midnight said.

The word *Luna* was still echoing down the hallway when a series of interlocking metal plates sprang from the bottom of Midnight's cowl. The pieces locked together over his mouth and nose, the only exposed areas in his mask. As this happened, two small launchers popped up from hidden recesses in the shoulders of his suit. Each ejected small canisters that were already spewing gas across the hallway floor.

Aria pulled the trigger.

Click.

Click. Click.

Nothing.

She coughed despite having held her breath the instant the canisters were ejected. She examined the gun and discovered the magazine was missing.

Midnight flicked the bullets out of the magazine in his hand one at a time, letting them clatter on the floor.

Confused and coughing harder, Aria dropped the useless gun. She reached behind her again and fumbled with her belt for another weapon, but before she could find one, she collapsed onto the floor, unconscious.

Midnight detached a small double-barreled cylinder from his belt, clicked a button on it, and dropped it to the floor. A motor inside whirred to life and vacuumed the gas out of the air. When the room's oxygen was safe to breathe again, the lower half of his mask retracted back into his cowl.

Midnight knelt beside Luna and placed two fingers to her carotid artery. The sensors in the glove's fingertips picked up her pulse and amplified the sound through small speakers inside his cowl. He didn't need to consult his other sensors to know she was alive and would recover. Gas was a tricky tool to work with, and one he did not care to utilize except in the most desperate circumstances.

He couldn't understand what had happened to the Luna he knew, but he told himself this wasn't the same woman, knowing full well that was a lie.

MIDNIGHT PICKED the lock of the door Luna had entered through. It wasn't especially difficult. He wondered if it was easy because no one had expected him to make it past a homicidal Luna or because Alastair had more challenges in store for him. Either way, he'd have his answer soon.

The strongly reinforced door opened to reveal the largest room yet. The large room resembled army barracks. Row upon row of bunk beds stretched in front of him, each stacked four beds high. The living conditions were much worse than any army barracks he'd ever seen, though. The beds were stacked so closely that he wondered how anyone even squeezed inside them.

Then he noticed the beds weren't empty. He quickly flipped through different augmentations on his visor and pulled up a heat map. Every bed in the large hall had at least one, if not two people crammed into it. There were hundreds of sleeping people in the room.

Grateful he'd entered the room quietly enough not to wake any of them, he scanned the room for an exit.

A door on the far wall likely led to the center of the compound. He hoped to find Amanda there so they could leave this place behind once and for all. Then suddenly, red lights flashed on and a deafening alarm blared, ensuring none of the sleeping residents could ignore it. The lights were so bright that they affected Midnight's visor. All he could see were alternating flashes of red followed by complete darkness. In between the darkness, he could see movement. Recognizing the danger he was in, the cowl disabled all vision enhancements.

"Intruder. Intruder," a monotonous voice droned through the PA system.

Midnight guessed it wouldn't take the inhabitants long to realize who that intruder was.

He ran for the door across the giant room. He was so fixated on reaching that door that he didn't see the tackle coming and hit the ground.

The man who had brought him down was much larger than Midnight. His size and weight had him pinned, and he struggled to reach a button on his gauntlet. The button was connected to a capacitor, which was connected to the battery unit that powered the computer system within his cowl and other features. Straining, he managed to reach the button and press it, sending a huge portion of the battery's power coursing through the suit's exterior all at once.

No matter how big the person was, 50,000 volts stung. The man instinctively rolled off Midnight, desperate to get away from the electric shock.

Midnight rose to his feet, panting for air. His cowl was offline from the electrical discharge, something he hadn't expected. He hoped the computer was rebooting, but the possibility that he'd completely drained the battery or caused it to short-circuit weighed heavily on his mind.

Not for long, though. The rest of the residents had kept a wary distance between them and Midnight after seeing what had happened to the large man, but they noticed that something was wrong as Midnight repeatedly tapped the side of his cowl and his gauntlet to bring the system back online.

They didn't all rush in at once. Only the brave and the foolish approached first. The first knucklehead rushed him and threw a wild haymaker. Midnight sidestepped it while still struggling to bring his computer system back online. As the man stumbled past, Midnight tripped him. He tumbled head over heels to the ground, but others were starting to feel more confident as they realized Midnight was without access to the gadgets that made him so dangerous.

A second man stepped forward and put his hands up in a fighting position, suggesting he had some training. The fighter feigned a right jab to see how Midnight would react and immediately followed up with a left one. Midnight barely reacted to the punches. Instead, he merely observed the man's style to determine the best course of action.

When the man took his passiveness as a sign of weakness, he threw a roundhouse kick.

This was a mistake.

Midnight caught the man's leg at the height of its arc, inches from his face. Then, in one fluid motion, he headbutted the man and swept his leg, leaving the fighter crumpled on the floor.

Midnight's cowl might be offline, but he could still knock a person out cold just fine.

What he couldn't do without it, though, was see the chair that someone from the growing crowd had thrown at the back of his head. The metal chair bounced off the back of his cowl. The cowl protected him from any damage, but the blow had thrown him off balance.

An unseen member of the crowd took advantage of Midnight's distraction and stomped down on his knee.

His knee bent in a way it shouldn't, and pain exploded through his entire leg. The leg gave out, and he fell to his knees.

The waiting mob didn't hesitate.

All at once they were on him, punching and kicking. He blocked the ones he could and tried to discourage others from getting close. He yanked the feet out from under potential combatants, sending them crashing to the floor.

The noses of the three closest to him were broken in quick succession. But the punches and kicks kept coming.

The crowd smelled blood in the water, and those on the outskirts saw their opportunity. The mob pulsed forward from all sides. Those closest to Midnight fell on him one by one. They clawed at his cowl, attempting to rip it off by force. A few sharp fingernails drew blood from his exposed cheek.

Soon, Midnight found himself on his hands and knees, desperately trying to keep his attackers off him. But there were too many. The ones at the back of the crowd were pushing harder and harder, piling onto the growing heap. The punches and clawing slowly stopped as the people on top of him were crushed by the surging crowd.

Midnight strained to stay on his hands and knees as more weight bore down on him. All around him was darkness.

In a last-ditch effort to free himself from the suffocating mob, he retrieved his grappling gun from his belt. Hands had been grabbing at it, but without knowing how to trigger the hidden release it was nearly impossible to remove. With the grappling gun in hand, he blindly pushed it upward through the bodies. People moved to avoid the sharp point of the grappling hook. Finally, he felt his hand hit open air. Before anyone could notice and push him back down, he fired.

Even through the bodies piled high on top of him, he heard the distinctive *clang* of the grappling hook hitting the ceiling and finding an anchor point. Midnight readjusted his hold on the pistol's grip, then he engaged the retraction mechanism.

The grappling gun burst to life, but its motor strained and its gears slipped. The muscles in his arm felt as though they were doing the same. He reached for another switch higher up, near where the safety would be on a traditional handgun. With the flick of his thumb, the overdrive mechanism engaged. The metal ceiling strained where the grappling hook was anchored, but it held.

Bodies tumbled off the mound faster and faster, then all at once as Midnight exploded through the top of the pile like he was shooting out of a volcano. A straggler held on to his leg long enough to go for a ride with him toward the high ceiling, and then he lost his grip and fell back onto the crowd.

As Midnight hurtled toward the ceiling, he cut the line. His momentum kept him traveling upward in an arc until the skylight came into sight. He retrieved another grappling hook from his belt and slammed it into the barrel of the gun. The hook engaged with the carbon fiber line cartridge in the handle with a click, and Midnight fired. The hook crashed through the skylight and kept going until it found an anchor point somewhere on the roof.

The swing reached its apex, and he used his free hand to fight off several cult members trying to bring him back down to the ground.

Finally, as he swung under the smashed skylight, he reengaged the retraction mechanism at maximum speed and the line sent him skyward. He pulled his limbs in close as he soared cleanly through the shattered window and out into the night sky.

Midnight detached the line and landed on his feet. He walked over to the smashed skylight and looked down. Below him, the zealots continued fighting and clawing at each other in confusion. Most were unaware that Midnight had left the building. It was best to keep them under that impression.

He walked along the roof toward a series of air conditioning vents. Alongside the ventilation ducts were a series of power and communication lines. He bent down beside one of them, produced a multi-tool from a pouch on his belt, and snipped it open. He then attached the exposed line to an open port on his belt. Sparks flew out of the line upon making the connection, but it accomplished what Midnight needed.

The surge of electricity forced a hard reboot of his suit's computer system. Slowly, it came back online, one component at a time. He kept the line plugged in to recharge the battery while he went through a series of diagnostic checks within his visor.

With the cowl's visor back online, Midnight scanned the facility from the rooftop.

Two buildings away, he spotted an unusual heat signature that was growing by the second.

That had to be where they were keeping Amanda.

SEVENTEEN

Midnight was now directly over the heat signatures. The power surge had damaged the system, though, and it was acting strangely. He decided it was best to be cautious and not rely on the readings, but until Amanda was safe, he didn't have much time to spare for caution.

The roof was without a skylight. Whatever Alastair kept in this room wasn't something he wanted visible from the outside. There was still one way in, though: the air ducts. Even a sealed room needed ventilation. It was one of the few constants Midnight found when facing impossible-to-enter spaces.

This space was big enough to require an air duct Midnight was confident he could fit inside. Given more time, he would have sent a telescopic camera in through the vent first to make sure he wasn't jumping into a stupid situation. Here, he was flying blind.

He used a tool from his belt to snap off the bolts holding the vent in place, then he ripped the grating from the air duct. Lowering himself down, he switched his cowl's visor from heat vision to night vision to navigate the dark corridor.

He'd crawled through enough air ducts in his day to feel confident that this one was sturdy enough to support his weight. He lowered himself onto his stomach and army crawled down the shaft. Crawling on his hands and knees would have been faster, but it also would have caused more noise, and noise was always the enemy of stealth.

Noise wasn't what gave him away this time, though. This time, it was a series of motion detectors and a pressure plate lining the bottom of the air duct.

Two steel walls shot down with enough force to sever a limb, boxing Midnight in.

He was trapped.

Without panicking, he removed a small torch from his belt and flipped it on. He aimed the white-hot flame at the bottom of the vent. Using a gas torch to cut through metal that was currently supporting his weight was tricky, but he had little choice. The torch quickly melted through the aluminum wall of the air duct, but unfortunately, that wasn't the only layer. Beyond the aluminum was another layer of thick steel. The torch turned the steel bright red but inflicted little damage. Meanwhile, the heat was building up fast inside the coffin-like tunnel.

"I'd recommend turning that off," a voice announced through a PA system.

Midnight immediately recognized the voice as belonging to Alastair Green.

"There's very little oxygen in there, and you don't want an open flame gobbling up what remains, do you?"

Midnight had come to the same conclusion and flicked off the torch. Alastair hadn't trapped Midnight to kill him; otherwise, such a warning would have been a waste of time.

The section of the air duct that Midnight was trapped inside detached and dropped. It hit the ground with a loud metallic clang. The two ends were once again open, the gates that had closed them off still attached to the rest of the ventilation system.

Midnight clamored out of the air duct and into a large, steel-barred cell.

On the other side of the bars was Alastair Green, in the flesh, grinning at his prize. He was flanked by armored guards. Other cells lined the walls of the large space, but all were empty—except for the one to Midnight's immediate right.

That one contained Amanda Khan.

"Amanda, are you okay?" Midnight asked as he rushed to the wall of bars separating them.

But she was unconscious.

"What have you done?" Midnight growled.

"That's a question that requires a fairly long answer, and frankly, I'm not sure I have the time required to answer it in full this evening."

"This is your last chance. Release me and this girl immediately," Midnight stated calmly.

"Last chance? That's a hell of a thing for a man to threaten whilst imprisoned, isn't it?"

"If you think I'm going to be in this prison for long, you don't know me very well."

"Quite the contrary, my friend. I know you very well, indeed. You see, I've watched you from afar for quite some time now. Part of me has always admired what you do and how you do it. To be human yet live in the world of metahumans for so long is no easy feat. And now, to have metahumans gone from the world again, I imagine it felt as though the proverbial rug was pulled out from under you. What are you to do now? Where are you to go in a world where your services are no longer required?"

"As long as there's garbage like you out in the world, I won't be looking for a new line of work anytime soon."

Alastair stepped closer to Midnight's cell. He glanced at the edges of the cell and Midnight's hands, seemingly double-checking that being this close was safe.

"I know we have our differences, Midnight. But perhaps there is some room for our views to overlap. I know you've struggled, as I have, to find your place in this world. What if I were to tell you there was a way to get it back?"

Midnight stared at Alastair but offered no response.

"The media has ignored me for far too long. They've written me off as a huckster and a fraud. No one has known about the work I've been doing until now. I haven't just sat back and offered my knowledge to the world. I've also sought out new knowledge. I have refused to believe there are aspects to metabands that we do not have the ability to understand. So while the rest of the world has ignored me, I have been hard at work. And now I've found the elements to unlock the true power hidden within these beautiful arti-facts. I have found the means to activate metabands once again."

Midnight listened intently while also scanning the room for a way out. He needed to understand Alastair's plan better to know what he was up against.

"You don't believe me," Alastair said. There was a tinge of disappointment in his voice. He'd long been insulated from those who didn't take every word that came out of his mouth as the truth. "I suppose I'll just have to offer you a demonstration."

Alastair motioned to the other men in the room. They

came forward to remove a covering from a table in the center of the room.

There, sitting on a pedestal, was Midnight's dampening device.

"You don't know what you're tinkering with," Midnight said.

Alastair's face broke into a wide smile. "So, it *is* true. You've seen this device before?"

Midnight did not respond.

"Of course you have. You've seen this device many times before because you created it, didn't you? I must admit, I didn't believe it myself when I first learned of its existence. It seemed too far-fetched. How on earth could a masked vigilante create a device powered by a metaband? How could he accomplish something every scientist on earth with access to metabands has tried for years and years without success? Yet here is a man who runs around rooftops, dressed all in black, who has found a way to not only draw power from a metaband, but also affect the powers of other metabands."

"You shouldn't be touching something you don't understand," Midnight said.

"I shouldn't? Well, that is quite the statement coming from you. You don't think I've put two and two together yet? You don't think I've figured everything out?"

"No, actually, I don't."

"Let me spell it out for you, then, shall I? This device was recovered from the site of The Battle, the last known time any metahuman has ever been seen using their powers. You came along with your little device and turned it on. Jones ripped through half the city before The Governor stopped him. Then, like someone flipping off a light switch, every metaband in the world stopped working at the same time, and you really expect me to believe that was all a coincidence? Of course it wasn't, and your device was to blame."

Midnight was silent.

Like the rest of the world, he didn't know for certain what had caused the metabands to cease working. Although he had ideas, they weren't anything he would share, especially not with Alastair. He was certain his device had had nothing to do with their failure, though. The machine simply wasn't powerful enough to affect metabands on that scale. It required a massive amount of energy just to disable the metabands within a thirty-foot radius. Affecting the entire globe just wasn't realistic.

What caused the metabands to fail was The Governor throwing Jones, and presumably himself, into the sun. There were no two ways about it. It was Occam's razor: metabands worked before Jones got thrown into the sun, and metabands stopped working after Jones got thrown into the sun.

"It really is a fascinating device," Alastair said. "How you melded this otherworldly technology with your own is truly a question that begs to be answered, but I suspect it isn't one you're eager to talk about. That's okay. We have ways of facilitating that conversation and making you more talkative."

On cue, men wearing lab coats appeared, entered Amanda Kahn's cage, and lifted her to her feet. She couldn't support her own weight as she drifted back to consciousness.

"You'll regret this," Midnight said.

"Not as much as you will, my friend," Green hissed back with a smile.

Midnight watched helplessly as the men dragged Amanda toward Green, while another set of men entered through a door on the other side of the room. They carried a collection of equipment, including what looked like a repurposed dental chair and an IV stand. The men placed Amanda in the chair.

"It took quite a bit of experimentation to power on this device again," Green said.

"It's useless. Metabands don't work anymore. All you're doing is lying to your followers and offering them false hope. You're a sick man."

"That's disappointing. I had hoped that a man of science like yourself would be more open-minded to the possibility that the device you created could still prove useful to this world.

"My hypothesis is as follows: your device caused the metabands to short-circuit, so to speak. However, I don't believe that was the true purpose of this device. Similar to how a defibrillator can stop the heart of a person who is not suffering from cardiac arrest and then restart that same heart moments later.

"The device you created to short-circuit active metabands turned out to be very useful in deactivating bands as well."

Midnight refused to believe what he was hearing. He'd created the device. He knew what it was and was not capable of. He knew it couldn't have deactivated metabands all around the world.

But there was much he didn't know. He'd lost the device in the aftermath of The Battle. There had been so much fallout, so much confusion and chaos in those days after the deactivations, that he hadn't given the device significant thought. It wasn't until almost a year later that he'd attempted to track it down, even though he figured it was useless.

Was Alastair speaking the truth?

"Now, the device is not without its limitations," Green said. "I'll be the first to admit that. Yet what it can do is miraculous, nevertheless. It makes me think of what might be possible with your assistance."

He was circling Amanda. He placed his index finger on her wrist, tracing the place where her metaband was once wrapped.

The men who had brought the equipment into the room left briefly and reentered with a small wooden box. They placed it on a table next to Amanda.

"You may have noticed we've made a few alterations to your device. I hope you don't mind. I figured the warranty likely expired anyway.

"The alterations made all this possible. The device, as originally intended, used only a single metaband as its power source. I'm not sure why you limited your vision this way. Perhaps you only had access to one working metaband at the time? Regardless, in my attempt to reboot this system and see how far I could push it, I came upon the idea of using both metabands tied to an individual. I'll admit, I'm quite embarrassed by how long it took me to think of this. Perhaps it's the same reason your thought process was hampered too. I've indeed upgraded the device, and as you'll soon witness, it is more powerful than ever before.

"I was concerned that it would be quite the undertaking to track down Ms. Khan's metabands. You can imagine my relief when we found them right under her bed, inside a shoebox of all things. Not really the safest place to keep some of the most powerful sources of energy in the known universe, if you ask me."

Alastair opened the box and removed a large, angular contraption. Inside the web of wires and structural braces,

Midnight spotted a pair of metabands. They were pushed together to form a tube of sorts, with clear plastic medical tubing running around each band.

Green took the mess of wires and cables and pushed them into the device Midnight had designed. It locked in place somewhat awkwardly, and Midnight noticed that pieces of his device were missing. Initially, he'd suspected they'd been damaged and knocked off in the chaos following The Battle, but Alastair had intentionally removed these pieces to fit the extra metaband.

"You have no idea what you're doing," Midnight said, feeling actual panic.

He was acutely aware of how powerful his device was. Much of the hardship in crafting it had involved ensuring its safety. If a metaband could feed a small percentage of its energy into the device, it could level a city.

The pieces Alastair had removed hadn't been ornamental. They were necessary to operate the device safely. And as Midnight had experienced firsthand, even then the device could react with metabands in unexpected ways.

"I know exactly what I'm doing, Midnight," Alastair said. "I'm bringing back metahumans to save the human race."

Green nodded to the men in lab coats, and they got to work.

First, they secured Amanda to the chair with a set of leather straps. Once the straps were tight, the men removed two long needles from sterile packaging. They attached the needles to the clear plastic piping wrapped around Amanda's dead metabands before inserting them into her arms. She winced as they pierced her skin, but she was too groggy to react beyond that.

Her eyes remained closed as the tubes turned from clear to red.

Midnight frantically searched for a way out, for a way to stop Green before he hurt Amanda any more than he already had, but he couldn't find one.

Yet.

As Amanda's blood coursed through the plastic tubing wrapped around his device, the metabands changed.

It was subtle at first, but within a few moments, it was clear they had taken on a different sheen. Midnight couldn't believe his eyes. Even while active, metabands were notoriously difficult to work with. The energy they tapped into couldn't be detected by modern equipment, and their effects differed from person to person. No one was even sure if it was the person or the metabands that determined the effect. After The Battle, it became even more difficult to experiment on or test metabands, which just added more credence to the idea that they were somehow magical or mystical in origin. A dead metaband was no different from one made of common metals, except even when dead, a metaband was still indestructible. This made cutting one open for study impossible.

But here Alastair was, using technology Midnight had built to cause a reaction with a pair of inactive metabands.

It had to be a trick. It was the same sleight of hand Green had used to build his army of followers. But even Midnight had to admit that something real was happening.

Alastair stepped forward, and a follower met him in the center of the room with a second wooden box. He flipped the lid open, revealing a second pair of metabands. Green ran his fingers over their exterior, admiring them. Then he carefully lifted them from the box and slipped them on his wrists.

"Did you ever hear how I found my metabands, Mr. Midnight?" Green asked.

Midnight didn't answer. He didn't care. He just wanted whatever was happening to stop so Amanda would be safe again.

"It feels like an eternity ago. It practically *was* an eternity ago when you look back at all that has changed. The place I was in then. The truths I had yet to learn. I'd reached the end of my rope. The industry I'd struggled to work for my entire life had told me they didn't want me anymore, that I was old news. They threw me out like yesterday's garbage. It didn't stop the bill collectors, though. The phone calls, day in and day out, telling me I owed money to companies I had never even heard of because my debt had been bought and sold so many times like scrap metal."

As Alastair Green told his story, Amanda's metabands began to glow brighter from within the device.

Then, the metabands around Alastair's wrists reacted as well.

They slowly tightened around his wrists. Not nearly as fast as they had when the world was rife with working metabands, but they were tightening. It was all impossible, but he had no reason not to believe his eyes.

"These soulless corporations hounded me. The money I owed was inconsequential. It didn't matter to them whether they got it back or not, but they went after everything I owned and stole it from me. The few times I scraped a few pennies together, they took it from me before I even saw it. There was no way out, so I decided to make my own way.

"That's how I found myself overlooking Empire City

Harbor on that night, sitting alone in my car. I was living out of it full-time, but the debt collectors told me they were going to take that from me too once they found it. They were going to find it, all right, and there was going to be a nasty surprise inside it when they did.

"So there on the bluff, I ran a garden hose from the exhaust in through the passenger side window. Can you believe I actually used the last twenty dollars I had on earth to fill up the gas tank? I was worried the engine would run out before the deed was done and I'd just wake up with a bad headache.

"No, if this was the last thing I did in my life, I would do it right. I fished the hose in through the window, closed it as tight as I could, and then stuffed the window gap with newspapers and other trash I'd found on the car floor. And then I turned the ignition and waited.

"It took forever before I started suffering any effects. Just coughing at first, but then I started feeling very sleepy. I thought I might have second thoughts or regret my decision, but all I felt was the overwhelming urge to sleep.

"And that's when he came to me. People always ask if it felt like a dream, but I know that's their way of trying to write off my experience. It's a way for those who feel uneasy about the unknown to feel more comfortable with their own doubt. It didn't feel like a dream. It felt like an awakening. Udo told me I wasn't done with this plane of existence and that my work had only just begun.

"That's when the windshield shattered. My connection with Udo was fading, and I assumed some Good Samaritan or firefighter looking to rescue me from my coffin had broken the windshield. But then I looked over to the passenger seat. The vision of Udo was no longer seated there, but his gift to me was. A pair of metabands had shattered the windshield and saved my life. And now it was my turn to place those metabands on my wrists and save the lives of so many others."

Alastair Green lifted his arms to his sides and then brought them together. The metabands clanged together and then activated. A long red and blue robe flowed out of them and enveloped Alastair's body as his feet levitated off the floor.

His metabands were working.

Amanda remained strapped to the chair, but she was writhing in pain, her eyes still closed.

Everyone else in the room fell to their knees and bowed to Alastair Green. His appearance had taken on a more regal, godlike image. He floated three feet from the ground and motioned his hands over them in a gesture of appreciation.

"You're no god. It's a trick. Can't you see that? You're all idiots and fools getting taken in by a false god who only cares about your money and allegiance," Midnight screamed through the bars.

"Shut your mouth!" the follower closest to Midnight yelled before quickly bowing his head again. He was gritting his teeth. Midnight had found his weak link.

"Shut my mouth or what?" Midnight shouted at the follower. "Your fake god will strike me down? If you want me to shut my mouth so badly, you'll have to do it yourself, you coward. But I'm warning you, you won't like how it goes for you."

"I've heard enough," another follower said as he rose to his feet.

Midnight hadn't been trying to goad him, but it was good enough. The follower hurried toward Midnight's cage.

Alastair ignored him, turning a blind eye to the violence inside the compound.

Midnight laughed at the man storming toward him, which only infuriated him more.

"Drop down to your knees, now!" the man screamed, his face red with anger.

Midnight laughed harder as he stood in the center of his cage, refusing to comply. The follower was right up against the bars of Midnight's cell, the blood vessels in his forehead near bursting.

"I said get down on your knees right—"

Midnight moved at superhuman speed. A black gloved hand thrust through the bars of the cell and grabbed the follower by his lapel as his mouth still worked to form the last syllable of his command.

With a firm grip on the man's jacket, Midnight yanked back, but unfortunately for the follower, the bars stopped his head from following. The cell rang like a bell, and the follower's knees buckled, but before he could hit the ground, Midnight unholstered the handgun from his belt.

"He's got Leonard's gun!" another follower screamed.

Midnight fired three shots.

Each bullet took out one of the overhead light fixtures. Only the soft light of Amanda's metabands, still firmly encased within Midnight's device, lit the room.

Shouts and scuffles filled the room as confusion took hold. Mixed in with the noise was the sound of a handgun's magazine and metal pieces hitting the tiled floor one by one.

Then the jail door creaked open.

EIGHTEEN

Midnight didn't intend this to be a fair fight, and it wasn't. The sole thing on his mind was saving Amanda. And the quickest way to save her was to dispatch of Alastair Green's followers as quickly as possible, and that meant fighting dirty.

He was moving so fast he didn't even bother switching his cowl's display to night vision. It was unnecessary. As the lights went out, he'd memorized the position of every person in the room. When a room suddenly goes dark, the natural human instinct is to stop in your tracks. You don't want to move around blindly and risk tripping or knocking into something. That wasn't what Green's men did, though. They came right at Midnight.

It was almost too easy for him to take them down in quick succession. They practically lined up for their beatings. All the while, Midnight was moving toward the center of the room, where Amanda was strapped to the chair.

When the onslaught stopped, he detached a small light coated in adhesive from his belt and hurled it upward. It hit the ceiling and stuck. Once in place, the light flashed on and illuminated the room. Midnight had shielded his eyes, but anyone who hadn't would be blinded for a few seconds.

The last-standing follower froze in place to Midnight's right. While everyone else had rushed Midnight, this man had played it safe and hung back. As he viciously rubbed at his eyes to clear his vision, Midnight knocked him out.

Up against the far wall, another man cowered in the corner. He had his hands up over his head for protection, a position that had spared him from the light's flash. Shivering in fear, he slowly lowered his hands and looked at Midnight.

Midnight squinted at him, and the man ran.

He tallied the unconscious bodies on the floor. Three were missing, including Alastair Green.

The fallen followers had been a diversion to get Alastair out of the room unharmed. The other missing two had escorted Green out of the room.

He approached Amanda and began uncoupling her from the chair. As he did, he glanced over at the pedestal where his device had sat. It was gone, along with Amanda's metabands. This was why Alastair hadn't joined the fight despite being powered up. His primary concern was keeping the device out of Midnight's hands.

Amanda was groggy, but she lifted her head and looked at him.

"Don't speak. Save your energy," he said.

He hurried to take the IVs out of her arms. From his belt, he retrieved a bandage that looked like synthetic skin, adhered it to where the needles had been inserted into her veins, and applied pressure.

"We're getting you out of here."

Midnight carefully began to lift Amanda from the chair, but to his surprise, she resisted his efforts. He gave her a confused look and tried again, but again she fought against him.

"I know you're in pain, Amanda, but we have to go. Goons are going to fill this room any second now, and the longer we stay, the worse it will be, so you have to listen to me."

"No ..." Amanda barely got out.

"Amanda, please ..."

"Not without Lily," she whispered.

"Lily? Lily is here, in the compound?"

Amanda nodded.

"I'll come back for her, but we have to get you out of here."

Amanda shook her head, and tears welled in the corners of her eyes. "No, they're going to kill her."

"I don't understand ..."

Amanda took a hard swallow to lubricate her dry throat. "She's in the basement with the others. He'll use her for the machine now that he can't use me anymore. He won't stop this time, even if it kills her."

This stopped Midnight in his tracks.

His priority was saving Amanda, but his conscience wouldn't let him sacrifice Lily.

It was time for a new plan.

He tapped a series of commands into the terminal on his wrist computer before grabbing Amanda's chair and dragging it across the floor. The chair was heavy and not meant to be moved with a person seated in it, but he managed it anyway. "What are you doing?" she asked, still struggling to regain her strength.

"Getting you out of the way while I make a new exit."

With Amanda on the opposite end of the room, Midnight retrieved from his belt a small metal sphere not too dissimilar to the one lighting the room. He turned a dial on the sphere and peeled back the adhesive, exposing a sticky substance.

Midnight stuck the sphere on the far wall. He pressed a button on the device and then briskly walked back next to Amanda. He stood in front of her, facing away from the wall, and knelt.

"Cover your ears," he told her.

"What?" she asked before remembering the rule about listening to Midnight's directions first and asking questions later.

And not a second too soon.

The sphere exploded and took out a chunk of the wall. Debris and smoke billowed toward Midnight and Amanda, but it was quickly sucked out of the room through the gaping hole in the wall that led directly outside.

"Come on, that'll draw some unwanted attention," Midnight said as he pulled her arm around his shoulders and lifted her.

They walked to the new entrance and carefully stepped through, Midnight leading the way. The air outside was noticeably colder. Amanda couldn't resist taking a deep breath to fill her lungs. She could already feel her strength returning.

Once they were outside and away from the smoke and debris hanging in the air, she saw where they were heading.

A black van.

As they approached, the side passenger door slid open silently, revealing the blinking lights and glowing screens inside.

"What is this?" Amanda asked.

"It's mine, and it's taking you home. It's preprogrammed and safe. All you have to do is rest."

Midnight lifted her into the van and placed her in the chair in the cargo area.

"What do you mean it's preprogrammed? You mean this thing can drive itself?"

"Yes."

"No," Amanda said and began struggling again. "I won't let you send me home before my friend is safe."

She attempted to move past him, but he remained immovable. Within a few seconds, she had worn herself out and needed to return to her seat.

"Just close the door and I'll wait here until you find Lily. Then we'll all go home together."

"I can't do that, Amanda. They're looking for us, and it's just a matter of time before they find us. Even with the van in lockdown, it's not impenetrable. The safest place for you is as far from here as we can get you and fast."

"No, I'm not leaving my friend!"

"Amanda. You're hurt. I know you want to help, but you can't. And I can't let you stay here when you're in danger. If Alastair finds you again, he won't hesitate to kill you. You understand that, don't you?"

"I don't care."

"Well, I do care, and if you care about Lily, you'll make sure I can focus on finding her. I can't do that if you're in danger."

Amanda thought about it, racking her brain for an excuse or argument, but there were none. He was right, and even if she didn't want him to care about her, he still would. She wasn't happy about it, but she had to listen to him for Lily's sake.

Amanda gave a quick nod and said, "Fine," barely above a whisper.

Midnight met her eyes. "I will find her, Amanda. I promise you."

Fresh tears welled in Amanda's eyes when Midnight stepped back from the sliding door. As soon as he was clear, it slammed shut, and the engine roared to life.

Just then, a bullet ricocheted off the van's bulletproof exterior. Midnight swung around to find a group of heavily armed guards approaching from across a field.

"Go!" Midnight shouted into his wrist computer.

The van's wheels spun as they tried to gain traction in the wet earth. The van wasn't meant for off-road expeditions. Midnight couldn't even remember the last time he'd left Empire City. The copious amounts of equipment weighing it down certainly didn't help either.

"Dammit," he said, frustrated by his own lack of planning.

The van was smart, though, and would stop at nothing to return to the city. Now it was just a question of it clearing the area before reinforcements arrived.

Midnight tapped another command into his wrist computer, and a small periscope emerged from the protective covering on the van's roof. It swiveled around and launched two projectiles in quick succession.

The first was a flash-bang grenade, which landed in the middle of the advancing reinforcements. These typically worked best in confined spaces, but they would work in a pinch. The second projectile landed and burst into a cloud of thick, black smoke.

The countermeasures worked, and the guards stopped shooting at him and the van.

As the smoke filled the field, Midnight rushed to the front of the van, where he detached a section of the front grill and pulled out a winch. He ran it to the nearest sturdy-looking tree and wrapped it around the trunk, then attached the line to itself.

Once in place, the winch retracted automatically, pulling the van. As soon as the van was free from the mud's grip, the winch detached and the van took off, driving fast toward the nearest access road.

Amanda was safe.

It was time to find Lily.

NINETEEN

Midnight scanned the compound's perimeter for movement. He expected to see a flurry of activity. The base was large, and evacuating it wouldn't be easy.

But there was no evacuation. Despite Midnight's infiltration, Alastair Green and his followers didn't panic. Why weren't they leaving?

He was grabbed from behind and lifted into the air by his collar. Another hand grabbed his other shoulder and spun him around.

It was Alastair. Even though he was a couple of inches shorter than Midnight, here he was, comfortably holding Midnight in the air, his feet dangling six inches off the ground.

"Looking for someone?" Alastair asked.

In quick succession, Midnight's suit deployed a variety of countermeasures. There was a bright flash and a loud pop, and then gas sprayed into Alastair's face from a hidden compartment in the suit's chest. None of these measures had any effect. The suit released an electrical discharge to loosen Alastair's grip.

"Stop, that tickles," he said.

The suit's defenses had all been triggered automatically when Alastair lifted him off the ground. The suit was smart enough to know what Midnight knew: he was in deep shit.

"I assume you didn't decide to stick around instead of leaving with your little friend because you had a change of heart and chose to join us," Alastair said.

"How?" Midnight asked.

"How what? How am I overpowering you so completely? It seems your little device has some residual effects. It doesn't last long, mind you. In a few minutes, these powers will be gone again, unfortunately. You never had powers so you can't possibly understand how addictive they are. Although I suppose you wanted them badly enough to dress up like a shadow and go running around rooftops at night.

"These effects are only temporary. That is until I hook up another acolyte to your wonderful invention."

"Amanda wasn't your acolyte."

"Who? Oh, the girl just now. You'll have to excuse me, I don't make much of an effort to remember their names after I'm done with them. To me, she's just another battery. Your device took the last bit of her energy and gave it to me all at once. It's no substitute for the real thing, but it's a hell of a lot better than nothing. The girl is all used up, though, so into the trash she goes with the rest of them."

Midnight struggled to break free of Alastair's grip, but it was futile. He hadn't dealt with a metahuman in a year, but he hadn't forgotten how strong they were—one of the reasons he concentrated on tactics that didn't involve hand-to-hand combat.

"Come now, Midnight. You've been at this long enough to know you can't squirm your way out of my grip. If you really wanted to avoid all this nastiness, you should have gotten into that van with your friend and headed back into the city. You could have gone on with your life, and we could have gone on with ours."

"You're a monster. You've brainwashed these people, used their deepest fears and desires to trick them into doing whatever you tell them while handing over all their money."

"Are you quite done yet?"

Alastair's grip slipped, and Midnight's feet almost touched the ground. But it was short-lived. He readjusted his grip and lifted Midnight even higher.

Taking his chance, Midnight brought both feet up and kicked off Alastair's chest, attempting to loosen his grip, but it was still no use.

"Oh, nice try there. As you noticed, it would seem my powers are failing. It's such a fleeting return to glory. Still, better to experience glory temporarily than never at all. We will have to figure out how to get rid of you, though. Can't risk having you here when my powers recede. Do you have any requests about how you'd like to go?"

Midnight said nothing, not wanting to give Alastair the satisfaction of giving up.

"Ah, I think I've got it," Alastair said as he readjusted his grip once more.

His powers were waning. He wasn't caught off guard like last time, but he had maybe a handful of seconds left.

"An oldie but goodie. It'll let me drag this out a little longer before you have to go, and the added bonus for you is that you get to experience what it's like to be a metahuman as well. You also get to experience death the same way they did." Alastair brought Midnight in close and whispered, "Up, up, and away."

Alastair's bicep and forearm flexed, and Midnight was flung into the air.

Green had thrown him with all his metaband-enhanced might.

The wind whipped past Midnight's face as he climbed higher. He had to turn his head just to gasp for air.

Below him, Alastair and a handful of followers grew smaller and smaller as he climbed into the night sky. Beneath him, the forest stretched endlessly. The moon was back out now and visible over the horizon.

He estimated he was roughly five thousand feet high before his ascent slowed. He was panicking at the loss of control and running through a list of scenarios and options to save his life, but he was coming up empty. The gauntlet he'd endured to find Amanda had damaged much of his suit and expended its energy.

Added to that, Midnight didn't have much of the gear he used when leaping across rooftops. He hadn't thought he'd need it against Alastair in his relatively flat compound. He hadn't expected any buildings taller than three stories, and although he liked to be prepared, the equipment he used to navigate rooftops and skyscrapers added unnecessary weight.

He'd run out of options, and this would be his final regret in a lifetime full of them.

As he fell back down to earth, he reached for the grappling gun on his belt. It would be of little use. The surrounding trees weren't tall enough to slow his descent effectively, even if he managed to hit one, and by the time he was close enough to fire, he'd have reached terminal velocity, and there simply wouldn't be enough altitude to slow down without ripping his arm off. Still, his basic drive to survive stopped him from accepting his fate.

He wouldn't go out having given up.

His cowl had enough power to keep basic operations online. He looked down, and through the infrared night vision, he saw Alastair staring up at him with a huge smile on his face.

Midnight's cowl sensors didn't spot the approaching van through the forest's thick canopy until it was just yards away from Green. The followers standing near him had just enough time to leap out of the way, but not Green.

He was so enraptured by the death plunge he'd set Midnight on that he didn't take his eyes off him until it was too late.

The front of the van slammed into Alastair at well over seventy miles per hour, according to Midnight's heads-up display. The collision sent Green soaring across the clearing. His body slammed into an oak tree with a sickening thud.

Whatever invulnerability he had siphoned out of Amanda had run its course.

The van screeched to a halt. The side door slid open, and Amanda emerged. She turned her head skyward. She'd seen what Alastair Green had done and found Midnight falling through the night sky.

Amanda didn't scream, though. She reacted.

She raised both arms, pointing them in Midnight's fast-approaching direction.

Then she closed her eyes and focused with all her might.

Leaves swirled around her. Then dust from the ground kicked up into the air. She squinted her eyes closed harder and pushed through her exhaustion, focusing.

Then, very clearly, two cones of air swirled from her

palms. They extended outward, higher and higher into the air.

With Alastair dead, the residual energy he'd siphoned from her returned, but without her metabands it would only be temporary. She strained to hold on to the energy with all of her might for just a few more seconds before it disappeared again forever.

Midnight was still hundreds of feet up and falling fast when he felt the change in air pressure against his skin. It was subtle at first, but soon, the gusts emanating from Amanda were pushing hard against his body, straightening him out and slowing his descent.

Through the swirling rings of air and forest debris, he saw the strain on Amanda's face as she struggled to hold on. She dug down deep and let out a guttural scream. Midnight felt his descent grind to a halt. He was still quite high off the ground, but he was close enough.

He aimed his grappling gun at the top of the nearest tree and squeezed the trigger. A grappling hook launched from the barrel and found its target. The cushion of air beneath Midnight vanished, and he was again falling.

The line between his grappling gun and the top of the tree pulled taut, and Midnight held on tight. He swung in a wide arc, nearly scraping the forest floor, and continued toward the sky. He released the line before reaching the pinnacle of his arc and landed in a heap on the ground.

The impact was brutal, but he was alive.

He put aside the pain and rose to his feet. He limped across the clearing, his hand on his side that had taken the brunt of the impact. The limp slowed him down, but his determination kept him going until he'd reached Amanda. She'd collapsed in front of the van's headlights. He scooped up her limp body.

"Amanda," he said, sounding panicked. "Amanda!"

Her eyes fluttered open and found his. He placed her on the ground, and without concern for who might be nearby, he ripped off his cowl.

"You're alive. Thank God."

"I wish I were dead," she groaned.

"I told you to get to safety."

"That's a nice way to thank someone for saving your life."

He'd been close to death many times, but never as close as tonight. He'd never felt so helpless. For a man who prided himself on self-reliance, it was a humbling moment to have someone else snatch him from the clutches of death.

"But why?" he asked.

"You didn't give up looking for someone I care about, so I wasn't going to give up on you."

Before Midnight could protest, Amanda flung her arms around his neck and hugged him. It had been a long time since someone had done that, and it felt good.

TWENTY

A late-night hiker miles away was the one who'd called the police. Years earlier, if someone had called the police to report a flying man, they would have been laughed off the phone. A few years later, they would have been told, "Who cares?" and hung up on. But today, a man spotted flying in the sky was cause for concern and would be met with a visit from the local sheriff.

The sheriff found Alastair Green's lifeless body among a throng of mourning followers. The man who had claimed to be a living god had not fared too well against a panel van, which was enough for even the most evangelical follower to question their faith.

Midnight and Amanda had found Lily. She'd survived Alastair's siphoning of her energy, but she was still an ardent believer. That changed the moment she saw his lifeless body and heard what he'd subjected Amanda to.

Lily cried and begged Amanda to forgive her, but she didn't need to. Amanda forgave her instantly. All she'd ever wanted was to have her best friend back in her life.

Flashing red and blue lights lit up the forest. The sheriff had called for backup, and from the number of approaching vehicles, they had taken him very seriously.

"Looks like it's time for me to go," Midnight told the two girls.

"We're not coming with you?" Amanda asked.

"No. They'll want to take formal statements from you. It'll help build a case against Neil and the others who facilitated Alastair's deception for so long. And you both need proper medical attention."

The distant flashing lights were joined by the growing wail of sirens.

"Thank you, Simon," Amanda said.

Midnight nodded in appreciation.

"Ah, screw it," Amanda said and flung her arms around Midnight, hugging him tightly.

He hesitated before putting his arms around her and returning the embrace.

"Stay out of trouble," Midnight said.

"Unlikely, but thanks anyway," Amanda said.

A flashlight beam fell over Amanda's face, and she let go of Midnight to shield her eyes.

"Hey, are you two all right?" the approaching cop asked.

Amanda turned back to Midnight, but he was already gone.

OVER THE NEXT FEW HOURS, more and more law enforcement officials arrived on the scene as it became apparent this was a much larger case than they'd imagined. Many from The Receptive were taken to nearby hospitals for malnutrition and dehydration.

The coroner removed the bodies of the former metahumans Alastair Green had used as guinea pigs. Everyone else on the premises was taken out in handcuffs.

The FBI arrived not long before the camera crews. The police questioned Amanda and Lily before bringing them to the closest hospital. Lily was suffering from dehydration and would need rest to recover from her ordeal.

The crime scene swarmed with activity for hours as witnesses and suspects were questioned and evidence was cataloged. Eventually, everything remotely interesting had been examined, and many of the law enforcement officers headed back to their offices to begin the paperwork necessary to prosecute the crimes committed here.

But there was one officer who lingered. His focus was on the room where Alastair had activated Amanda's metabands through the misuse of Midnight's device. He'd been over the area multiple times with a set of tweezers, collecting samples of dust and debris.

"If you're going to watch me do this all night, the least you can do is say hello," the agent said, his attention still on the samples he was collecting.

Midnight stepped out of the shadows from a corner of the room but didn't speak.

The agent looked up at him. "I'm guessing this is as close as I'm getting to a hi."

"What are you looking for?" Midnight asked.

The agent rose off his knees and took off the latex gloves and his glasses. "A few witnesses told us about a strange device they saw operating in this room. The only thing is, we can't find a trace of it. You wouldn't have any idea about where it went, would you?"

"It's been returned to its rightful owner."

"Well then, that's good to hear. Wouldn't want something like that getting into the wrong hands."

"And who decides which hands are the wrong ones?"

The agent smiled. "Who knows anymore."

"You're not FBI."

"What gave it away?"

"You've barely interacted with the other law enforcement officers on the scene, and you're singularly obsessed with this area of the crime scene. You're not investigating the crimes that happened here. You're interested in the technology."

"It's that obvious, huh?"

"Who do you work for?"

"I'm not at liberty to divulge that information, but I can assure you I work on the side of the good guys too."

"Everyone always thinks they're on the side of the good guys."

"That's true, but I'm sure whatever side I'm on, our interests are aligned. The name's Halpern." He extended his hand for Midnight to shake but was left out to dry. "Anyway, I'm glad to see you're still alive and well. A few of us were concerned after The Battle when there weren't any sightings."

"Sightings usually mean I'm not doing my job well."

"I see eye to eye with you there. I'm going to call you figuring out I'm not FBI and me figuring out you were over there hiding in the corner for the last hour a draw on that count. I am glad I didn't scare you off, though. I hadn't counted on meeting you tonight, but since you're here, maybe I can convince you to work with us—"

Midnight glared at Halpern.

"—from time to time," Halpern continued. "I know you're a busy guy, so I don't expect you to turn in the mask and tights for a nine-to-five anytime soon, but you could still be a tremendous help to us. The world thinks our metahuman problems ended after The Battle, but that couldn't be further from the truth. The fights might not be happening in the sky anymore, but my ... agency has been busier than ever, and we could use the help."

"And what's in it for me?" Midnight asked.

Halpern smiled.

"The same thing that's always in it for you: nothing. We both know if you wanted something out of this, you would have given it up a long time ago, but here you are."

Midnight said nothing.

"There are still bad people out there, and The Battle hasn't stopped them from leveraging metabands and metahumans to accomplish their goals. Tonight, your device proved that metabands aren't as dead as everyone thought."

"Careful," Midnight said.

"Don't worry. It's in our best interest to keep this under wraps. We're lucky that most of the witnesses to tonight's fireworks display were brainwashed members of a cult, so they won't have too much success convincing outsiders of what they saw. This isn't our first rodeo. There have been other ... incidents that we've kept out of the public eye."

"Such as?"

Halpern smiled again. "I would love to tell you all about them, but I'm sure you more than anyone can understand the need for a few secrets now and then. Now, if you were willing to share some information with me about the device that was here, I might change my mind."

Midnight turned without hesitation and walked toward the blasted-out hole in the wall.

"Ah, that's what I thought. It was worth a shot."

Midnight hesitated. If there were other metabands out

there that were active or being used for other means, he had a moral obligation to get involved.

"I'll be in touch," Midnight said.

"I'm sure you will," Halpern replied.

Midnight stepped through the hole in the wall and disappeared into the night.

THANK YOU

Thank you so much for taking the time read my book. If you enjoyed it and would like to leave a review about it on whatever Internet website you bought it from it would mean the absolute world to me and make sure that there's more. If you bought the book at an actual store, wow. I guess you can go to the store and tell the nice man or woman that sold it to you how much you enjoyed it.

To stay in the loop on all things 'Meta' and otherwise with me, please sign up for my mailing list at tomreynolds.com/list. You'll get the first chapters of any new books before anyone else and other fun stuff early. No spam either, I promise.

ABOUT THE AUTHOR

Tom Reynolds lives in Brooklyn, NY with a dog named Ginger who despite being illiterate continues to prove to be a really great late night writing partner.

tomreynolds.com

twitter.com/tomreynolds

instagram.com/tomreynolds

facebook.com/sometomreynolds

bookbub.com/authors/tom-reynolds

goodreads.com/tomreynolds

amazon.com/author/tomreynolds

ALSO BY TOM REYNOLDS

Meta (Meta: Book 1)

The Second Wave (Meta: Book 2)

Rise of The Circle (Meta: Book 3)

9 781717 012531